THE BEHEADING GAME:

AN ARTHURIAN TALE

by

BARAK A. BASSMAN

TELEMACHUS PRESS

THE BEHEADING GAME: AN ARTHURIAN TALE

The publisher does not have any control over and does not assume any responsibility for author or third-party websites or their content.

Cover designed by Telemachus Press, LLC

Cover art Public Domain

Published by Telemachus Press, LLC
7652 Sawmill Road
Suite 304
Dublin, Ohio 43016
http://www.telemachuspress.com

ISBN: 978-1-951744-71-7 (eBook)
ISBN: 978-1-951744-72-4 (Paperback)

Library of Congress Control Number: 2021908380

Version 2021.04.26

Table of Contents

THE BEHEADING GAME:
AN ARTHURIAN TALE

I. The Challenge

IT WAS DURING the Christmas festival that Sir Carados took the oath that would ruin his life. Before then, he had been fortune's darling: the handsome and dashing only son of a powerful lord, he had jousted so well at a tournament earlier that year that no less a worthy than Sir Lancelot had made him a knight. Triumph had followed triumph, and his greatest worry was which ravishing, highborn maiden to pick as his bride.

And thus the young Sir Carados was not surprised when he was invited to King Arthur's court for the Christmas festival. He rode straight from his father's castle to Camelot, whistling merrily through the gently falling snowflakes. When he arrived, Arthur greeted him like a long-lost brother and sat him in a place of honor in the sumptuous hall.

But then everything changed on Christmas Eve. After spending the day hunting in the forest, Carados greedily sniffed the fresh boar meat cooking on the spits. His stomach twisted painfully with hunger, and the hunger in turn made him irritable and impatient.

Yet he now discovered a custom of King Arthur that had long been the bane of Camelot's knights: During festivals, when he had gathered his court in full force, Arthur would not permit any-one to eat until he saw or heard about some worthy marvel. The starving and ill-humored knights had been known more than once to stage fake wonders or tell wild, extravagant lies to satisfy this ridiculous royal caprice.

This Christmas Eve, however, required no such underhanded trickery. As the sun was setting and reddish light reflected through the windows onto the ladies' silk gowns, there was suddenly a loud commotion—sounds of futile protest and indignant yelling from outside the hall, followed by loud, plodding hoofbeats on the stone pavement. A couple of minutes later the doors to the hall burst open and in rode a massive horse, which was as big as three of the chargers typically ridden by Arthur's knights. Even more remark-able was the rider: He was as tall and as wide as two men put to-gether, and his bare head almost touched the high ceiling. His red hair and beard fell messily down below his shoulders, and he wore a dark green cloak over a dark green hauberk. But he bore no shield or lance or sword; his only weapon was an enormous axe belted to his hip.

The knights and ladies in the hall fell silent. For several minutes the giant sat smug and mute atop his horse, calmly looking down at the glittering court of Camelot.

Finally, King Arthur stood up and forced a smile. He greeted the strange knight in Christ's name and offered him blessings and good tidings.

The giant did not reply.

Arthur offered to stable his horse, invited him to join the feast, and suggested he could hear Christmas Mass that midnight in the Church of St. Stephen.

The giant still did not reply.

After a lengthy pause—during which Carados acutely felt the sharpness of his hunger pangs—Arthur asked if there was any favor that the stranger wished to request of him; if it was within his power, and would bring no shame or dishonor, the king would gladly grant the giant his heart's desire.

Now the giant spoke at last: I do have a favor to ask, Your Majesty. I wish to test the worthiness of your knights.

As long as your challenge involves no base conduct, King Arthur said, go ahead and state your terms. The finest knights in my kingdom are gathered here tonight.

The giant smirked, dismounted, and then raised his axe over his head.

Assembled knights, he began, hear my challenge: I ask one of you to take this axe from my hands. I will then kneel before you, and you may strike one blow. I will not flinch or run or resist in any way. And then, one year from today, in this very same place, you will kneel before me and permit me to strike one blow in return upon your head. Who shall accept my challenge?

Carados thought: Once the challenge was accepted and the axe was swung, Arthur would finally let everyone eat, as this was surely a worthy marvel. He twitched with excitement at the thought of tearing at the succulent, roasting meat with his teeth.

But no champion stepped forward. Each of the famous knights assembled in that hall—Lancelot, Gawain, Bors, Hector, Tristan, Palamedes—stared at his feet and appeared to try to fade into the tapestries on the walls.

Carados could not understand why no one would grab the axe and sever that arrogant head from its hulking body. Spurred on by sharp pinpricks of hunger, he felt angrier and angrier at the cowardly knights around him. Had they no sense of honor? What did they fear? After all, many of them had vanquished giants who had fought against them. What was so terrifying about this giant who apparently wished to be cut down like a sheep for the slaughter?

Losing his patience, he shoved his way forward, and shouted out: Give me the axe and I will gladly strike you the last blow you will ever feel.

Very good, very good, said the giant. I had hoped a more famous knight would accept my challenge, but I suppose the renowned names assembled here are attached to the hearts of pitiful cowards. So, it shall be you, boy.

Carados reached for the axe.

Wait, the giant continued. I need to be sure you will keep to your side of the bargain and return next year to submit to my blow. I demand you swear an oath, before all assembled here, upon holy Christian relics: You will return to this spot a year from today and kneel before me and take my reciprocal blow to your head with this axe.

King Arthur nodded gravely and dispatched a messenger to the Church of St. Stephen. Shortly thereafter, the messenger returned with a priest carrying sacred relics—the bones of a saint martyred during the persecutions of Diocletian—who administered the oath to Carados. Consumed with impatience and hunger, he quickly agreed to whatever the priest intoned without listening too closely to the words being said.

Now the giant handed the axe to Carados and submissively knelt before him. Carados swung the axe down upon the giant's neck and severed his head in one blow. He then tossed the axe aside and watched the head roll across the floor. He smiled with satisfaction in the knowledge that he was at last going to eat.

But then his smile disappeared, and his heart became heavy with dread: Instead of falling to the ground, lifeless, in a pool of blood, the headless body had remained in the same kneeling position, as if it were still alive—and it was not bleeding.

A moment later the headless body stood back up of its own accord, walked past Carados, and picked up its head. The head now opened its eyes again and looked at Carados. It spoke to him in a booming voice: Knight, you have struck your one blow. I shall see you again a year from now, here in this hall, where I shall strike my blow in turn.

Then the body put the head back in place atop its neck and the once more intact giant mounted his huge horse and rode away.

Carados now stood in stunned silence; he had lost his appetite.

II. The Drowning of Sorrows

RATHER THAN RETURN to his family's castle after the Christmas celebrations, Carados lingered on in Camelot, lodging in a dirty room in a dingy inn. He was not sure what to do with himself now that he would be dead in just under a year's time. No beautiful lady would marry him under such grim circumstances, and he would certainly sire no heir.

Nor did new adventures tempt him. He considered arming himself and riding out to meet the most dangerous foes in the forests of Logres—to the lairs of dragons and giants, to wizards who enchanted and robbed passing strangers, to rogue lords who abducted pretty maidens and imprisoned them in dungeons; after all, quite soon he would be dead no matter what, and maybe he could win some glory for himself and his family.

But he could not summon the strength to rise from his table and put aside his jug of mead. He found it hard to care about glory in which he would not be able to revel. When in the past he had dreamed of performing magnificent deeds, he would picture himself receiving the cooing, gushing praises of Queen Guinevere and the other ladies of the court. Or he would see himself as an old man in his father's hall, lord of the castle, basking in the abject adoration of his wife, children, and vassals while a groveling but talented minstrel sang of Carados's heroic feats as a brave young knight.

But now he saw himself bleeding to death outside a dragon's cave, his hauberk shredded by its claws and his abdomen torn to bits. Even if he somehow killed the terrible beast, he would never be celebrated for it. His body would never be found and would be food for slithering worms and eager maggots.

Thinking these melancholy thoughts as he sipped his mead, Carados noticed that the people of Camelot were keeping their distance from him. The innkeeper and his wife were huddled in one corner. Over there, on the far other side of the tavern, he saw a gathering of merchants. Passing by the window outside were knights and squires on various errands. But no one would speak to Carados. He caught them stealing glances at him and whispering, but they avoided his company as if he carried a pestilence—as if his foolish oath to the giant, which guaranteed his forthcoming death, were somehow contagious.

Several days passed this way, brooding and drinking, until a priest approached him. Knight, he said, you must turn your eyes away from the things of this world and submit meekly to the fate you cannot change. Come with me, confess, repent, and prepare your soul to meet its Creator and to be judged in the next world.

Lacking any better notion of what to do with his time, Carados, already half-drunk that morning (although it was only the hour of terce), followed the priest to the Church of St. Stephen. With the Christmas holiday over, the vast cathedral now appeared empty and desolate. Next to the altar was a statue of Jesus on the cross, his face drawn and deathly pale, and his big, anguished eyes looking out onto the rows of deserted pews. Carados wondered how this wooden Christ made it through the long, lonely seasons when no one kept him company.

Confess, Sir Carados, you must confess and unburden your heart to God. Confess, and seek forgiveness for your many sins.

Carados nodded. He would sincerely confess and cleanse his soul. The priest was right: His death was inevitable, and would be upon him before he knew it, and thus it behooved him to prepare for judgment in the next world. Better to enter Paradise than to burn in Purgatory.

The priest leaned forward. Carados started to speak but then faltered and fell back into silence. He was having difficulty confessing his sins, because he did not believe he had done anything wrong. He was supposed to train to become a knight, and he had done so. He had always been courteous to the maidens around him and never tried to shame them, either by guile or by force. While he had never been an especially religious man, he had been baptized and regularly enough heard Mass and took communion.

As he mulled upon his upright life, he grew ever more indignant at his unfortunate fate. There were many knights in Arthur's court who *had* shamed ladies to satisfy their lusts, or who had stolen from their vassals, or who had murdered for sport, just to prove they were stronger knights than their adversaries. Why weren't any of those men cursed to die in a year?

The priest again urged him to confess.

Carados replied that he had no sins to confess. If anything, he had been the victim of an unjust fate, sentenced to die even though many truly wicked knights would continue to roam the kingdom of Logres perpetrating their crimes for many years to come.

The priest looked at him sternly: Your words reek of overweening pride. We are all sinners. To say you have nothing to confess is to lie to your Father in Heaven, even though He knows all. When God asked Cain where his murdered brother was, do you think this was because the Heavenly Father had failed to witness Cain's horrible crime? No, it was because God wanted Cain to confess and to be contrite. And that is what He asks of you, too, Sir Carados, that you confess and be contrite.

There are many worse men than me. They should confess first.

The priest sighed and shook his head. God will not spare you from His holy wrath simply because others deserve punishment, too. And you *have* sinned. You tried to kill a man on Christmas Eve. He knelt before you, defenseless, and you swung an axe through his neck. Murder is a terrible sin. You must confess. You must repent.

Carados stood up, his blood now boiling with rage. How was it a sin, he said, to behead a giant who had challenged all the knights of Camelot to strike that very blow? When a knight brings forth a challenge, only a coward will shy away. If a knight were to challenge me in a clearing in the woods, would it be a sin for me to face him and run him through with my lance? Or are you saying that God's will is that we all be cowards, running away from every battle lest we be tarred with the sin of fighting to defend our honor?

And with that, Sir Carados stormed out of the church, seething with disgust.

Exhausted from this encounter, he returned to his inn and fell into a deep, dreamless sleep.

When he woke, it was nighttime. A bright white moon shone into his window, but otherwise the world was quiet and dark. His head throbbing, Carados decided he needed some fresh air to clear his mind.

He dressed quickly and went outside for a walk. The muddy streets of Camelot were deserted. Even the sentries in the watch towers seemed to have fallen asleep.

Carados ambled aimlessly through the narrow alleyways between low wooden houses and shops, until in the distance he spied a mysterious, dim red light. Without giving the matter much thought, he turned his steps in the direction of this red light and groped his way forward in the gloom. He felt as if he was travelling

on a downward slope, away from King Arthur's palace on the high
ground towards a submerged, distant corner of the city. As he
came closer, he heard sounds of laughter and music and the pour-
ing of drinks. His pounding temples yearned for another cup of
mead. He quickened his pace.

When he arrived at the red light, he found a closed door and
shuttered windows; the light was leaking out from their edges and
crevices, making a stark contrast to the gloom of the alleyway.

Carados banged on the door.

A familiar voice answered, slurring its speech: Who dares to
break down the gates and storm this fortress of pleasure? Know,
foul rapscallion, that I am a knight of the Round Table. I will
challenge you in King Arthur's name, you … you … you …

Then the door swung open with a violent jerk. Carados now
beheld Sir Mordred, son of Arthur's sister Morgause, swaying before him with a mad grin, a rumpled mantle, and a stench of stale
alcohol and vomit.

Oh, Sir Carados, it is you. Forgive me my disarray, my Lord,
and please come in, enjoy the fine hospitality of this glorious castle.

Mordred pulled him inside. The interior of the building was
filled with red, flickering lamps hanging from notches on the walls.
There were small couches, just big enough for two people, scattered about a vast room, where men and women, in sweat-soaked
clothes, were laughing and drinking together.

Mordred clapped his hand on Carados' shoulder and shouted
several times for quiet. When all eyes had finally turned to him, he
spoke: Dear, beloved friends, I wish to welcome my esteemed lord,
a man of great chivalry, Sir Carados. His chivalry is so great that
when all the rest of us had the good sense to decline a challenge
from a stranger that could only end in shame and dishonor and
decapitation, he boldly stepped forward, swore an irrevocable oath
upon the holiest relics, and now awaits the return of the giant who

will slice his pretty young head off. So, enjoy him tonight, I beseech you, because he will not be here with us much longer.

Mordred raised his cup high in the air, and then drank; the others did likewise. Carados thought that he should be angry—that he should want to strike Mordred for his mocking words—but the red lights and the strong smells of wine and sweat dulled his senses. His head had stopped pounding, although he still felt lightheaded and thirsty. He stepped forward, toward Mordred, but lost his footing and collapsed onto the hard marble floor; for a brief moment everything went dark.

When he came around, a woman helped him to stand up again. She was tall and voluptuous, with long red hair and red eyes and an elegant red gown that flickered amongst the red lights. Her face, while attractive, was not young—there were lightly etched wrinkles and lines on her skin—and her expression was demure and inviting.

She handed him a large cup and urged him to drink. It was mead, the sweetest and freshest he had ever tasted. He drained his cup to the dregs and asked for more.

Follow me, she said.

She led him down a long side corridor into a small room. Its walls were bare and pealing, except for the ubiquitous red lamps. There was a narrow, torn mattress in the center of the floor.

She said to him: The night can last as long as you wish. You will need to pay, but not right now. Sir Mordred has vouched for your high rank.

Then she disrobed.

The sight of her naked body jolted him out of his stupor. He suddenly felt disgusted by this place and this wrinkled hag of a whore. He threw his cup down to the ground and looked for the door. But it had somehow disappeared.

Let me out! he screamed at her. Get away from me!

She reached out and stroked his cheek. But don't you find me beautiful?

Let me out, get away.

She stepped back and lay down on the mattress in a languid, alluring pose. She spoke again: My Lord Carados, you know that, in just under a year, the giant will come back to Camelot and he will return your blow with his axe. But unlike him, you will not be able to put your severed head back onto your body. Your life is over. You will never marry. If you want to taste the pleasures of love, sin is your only path.

But to call it sin is wrong. You swore an oath on the Lord God's holy relics, but then He abandoned you to that monster. I am trying to give back what He took from you—the soft bliss of love that should have been yours on your wedding night. Take your delights now, boldly, courageously, and stop cowering in fear of the God and Church and King who have all abandoned and betrayed you.

But Carados was unmoved—he knew her favors were wretched and base. Even if he must die, he would do so with honor and dignity. Yes, he had been foully tricked, but he still could choose to face his fate bravely. His honoring of his terrible oath and his show of courage in submitting to the reciprocal blow would bring glory and renown to King Arthur and to his court. Poets would sing of his virtue.

His virtue: That is what he must safeguard. So, he would not touch this woman.

She tried another tack: I see you are still hesitating. You are worried about the sin and the fate of your soul. But you can outwit those who would condemn you for wanting what is only natural for a man to want. You know the very day when the axe will come down upon your head. You can sin as much as you wish—feel such wonderful things, seize whatever excites your eyes—and simply repent the morning of your death. As long as you repent before dying, all your sins will be forgiven, and your soul will ascend straight to Paradise. You can have all the pleasures of both this world and the next.

There is also no reason to worry about how the king and his court may judge your conduct. Once you are dead, they will forget you, regardless of how you have behaved. And why should anyone remember you? You will leave no heirs. And your one adventure will be meekly kneeling down and getting your head chopped off.

So come to me here, take and enjoy what is yours while you can.

Carados felt his fury rise at her words. How could she belittle his glory? To keep a sacred vow, when to do so leads to certain death, would be the greatest chivalry, a devotion to honesty and piety and goodness that could not be matched.

So, he said back to her, firmly: No. Let me leave.

She hissed in response and her body shook in an inhuman way.

When she had composed herself again, she said he would not be granted his leave until they had kissed.

Seeing no other way to escape, he reluctantly agreed to her terms.

You must come to me, she said.

Carados walked over to the mattress, knelt down, and leaned forward to her lips. But then he flinched. She grabbed his cheeks and pulled him into her, kissing him so intensely that he felt as if she were trying to suck his innards out from his chest. The world spun wildly, and then his body fell numb and he lost consciousness.

When Carados awoke, the sun was high in the sky and painfully bright. He was lying, nauseous and stiff, in a small pen with a pair of stunted, smelly goats. A crowd of peasants surrounded him, crossing themselves furiously and beseeching Heaven.

As he started to get up, he felt that he was stuck to something hard and rigid. Rubbing his eyes and looking down, he suddenly saw that his body was tangled with a skeleton with long red hair. Although he tried to pry himself loose, its bones had entwined themselves too tightly about his legs and feet, and he flailed helplessly in their grip.

Eventually two monks arrived who extricated Carados from the skeleton and gathered the bones in a sack. Then they led him away to their abbey, singing Latin hymns as they went.

Once inside the cloister, the good brothers lay Carados down in a proper bed and placed another monk by his side to read Psalms to drive away whatever infernal spirits had been haunting him.

After resting for a couple of days, he was ushered into a large reception room where he found his father and the abbot waiting for him. The abbot explained that, while Carados appeared to be free from demonic possession and had only suffered a slight chill in his chest from sleeping outdoors, the skeleton with which he had been entwined had proved to be far more concerning.

The abbot recounted that he had given the bones to an aged and deeply learned friar to examine. When an insect flew near the skeleton, the skull's jaws opened and chewed it. The good brother tried reciting an exorcism spell, but then the skull opened its jaws again and let out such a harsh shrieking sound that the friar fell to the ground in an agony of pain.

Terrified now, he threw the bones into a pit and burned them. The smoke rose to the sky in a dense red pillar. The friar swore he saw the smoke form into hideous and mocking faces, which looked human and yet somehow were not.

The abbot concluded his tale: Sir Carados, you have had congress with dark spirits, ungodly and wicked. Please, confess what happened and help us to root out this evil.

Embarrassed and ashamed, he lied and insisted he had no memory of that night.

Are you sure, my son? There is no profit in concealing your sins. Only forthright confession, contrition, and penance can cleanse your soul.

But Carados was adamant that he recalled nothing.

The abbot sighed and walked away. He said that he would leave Carados alone with his father, as he was sure they had much to discuss.

Once the abbot was gone, his father addressed him, eyes brimming with disgust: Carados, what has become of you? I saw you off to His Majesty's winter court as an honorable young knight, esteemed by all. Many great lords were then whispering in my ears about the charms of their daughters, about how those lovely maidens could please you and enhance your honor. I began to contemplate a marriage alliance that would grow our lands and influence—and you, a famous knight of the Round Table, at the head of our kin.

But then a messenger came to me from this abbey. I thought he was a madman: He claimed you had decapitated some kind of demon and swore an oath on holy relics to let the demon, who of course survived, cut off your head in turn in a year's time. And then you were found drunk and disheveled in some peasant's filthy yard, wrapped in the carnal embrace of a skeleton possessed by some hellish fiend.

I accused the man of lying and threatened to flog him. But he did not waver, and so I sent for holy relics. Once the messenger had sworn upon them that he had not lied, I knew that he believed himself to be telling the truth. But perhaps he was deluded? It simply could not be that you had tossed your life away so carelessly and then decided to shame yourself in public with a pile of bones.

So, I journeyed back to this abbey with the messenger. I also dispatched some of my vassals to ride ahead to Camelot on my swiftest horses. They returned to me with terrible news: the messenger's bizarre story was true, every word of it. And this morning, the abbot recounted those very same events to me.

How can this be? How did you abandon all reason and decent sense? Well, say something.

Carados looked at the ground. He tried to speak, but the words were caught in a sticky web at the base of his throat and could not ascend up to his lips. He felt an urge to tear his skin from his body. But instead, he closed his eyes and he felt tears involuntarily slither down his cheeks. He was ashamed to be crying like a pitiful, sniveling child but he could not stop himself.

His father walked over and touched Carados' tears with the tip of his forefinger. Then his father struck him hard across his face, sending him hurtling toward the floor.

You disgrace, he said, you have not only shamed yourself and our family, but you are too much of a coward to admit plainly what you have done.

And now? Well, I suppose the past is the past and what has happened has happened. You are fated to die from the demon giant's axe in a year's time.

But maybe you can die with some honor intact.

Stop moping about with these whimpering, womanish priests. Arm yourself as a knight should, seize a good horse, and seek adventures. Fight every knight or warrior or monster you can find. You need not fear death—death is coming for you, and quickly, no matter what you do. No, you should welcome death. Challenge brave and bold knights and die fighting valiantly.

The bards will then sing your praises. Suitors will beat down your sister's door, and her noble children, my grandsons, will boast of your lineage. You can still salvage something of your dignity. After all, is this truly what you wish to be—a drunken coward fornicating with dry bones?

Carados now stood back up and opened his eyes again. His father was right: He should seek daring adventures so he could die as a heroic knight errant. Although he had sworn to submit to the reciprocal blow, he had made no promise about how he would spend the intervening year. Why not seek the boldest adventures— challenge the strongest knights—dare death to seize him early. If he should die, then it will be a death full of glory.

Feeling reborn as a knight and as a man, he embraced his father and thanked him. He swore to ride forth that very day to seek out fierce battles and heroic deeds.

III. The Knight Errant

CARADOS LEFT THE abbey, returned to Camelot, and recovered his horse from King Arthur's stables. He then rode three days and nights through the forest without finding any adventure worth the telling, until he came to a bridge stretching across a river. On the far side was a castle, on the near side, a guard tower. Dozens of shields hung from the branches of a broad tree next to this guard tower—gold, silver, blue, green, and red, bearing emblems of dragons and wolves and lions and bears.

As Carados advanced towards the river, he was accosted by a scrawny peasant with a face like a rat, who rudely grabbed his horse's bridle and demanded he state his business.

To cross the bridge, good sir.

You cannot cross. This bridge belongs to my master, who forbids passage. I advise you to turn back if you value your life. Do you see those shields hanging there from the branches? Those knights also thought they could cross this bridge. Unless you turn around and go back the way you came, my master will knock you to the ground, and take your horse and shield.

Carados was overjoyed: He had finally stumbled upon a worthy adventure. So, he boldly issued a challenge: I *will* cross that bridge. If your master wishes to stop me, then I urge him to come forward now to joust and not to hide behind the boastful words of a sniveling vassal.

The peasant grinned maliciously and told Carados to wait where he was, before scampering off to the guard tower. Shortly thereafter an enormous knight in vermillion armor rode forth to meet Carados' challenge.

Their horses flew at one another. The other knight's lance splintered into pieces against Carados' shield, but the force of the blow still threw Carados to the ground. For a couple of minutes, he did not know where he was or if it was day or night. But then he regained his reason and stood back up. He pulled his sword from its scabbard, ready to continue the battle on foot.

But he did not see his adversary anymore. Approaching the guard tower, he came upon his opponent's overturned horse, which had pinned the vermillion knight to the ground. Blood was gushing rapidly out of the man's body, as Carados' lance had lodged deeply into his abdomen and then came out through his spine in the back.

Carados knelt down and removed the knight's helmet. The man's eyes had clouded over, and he was drooling from the side of his mouth. Carados asked him to yield, but the knight seemed not to hear.

Carados carefully pulled his still-intact lance out of the man's body and asked again if his opponent yielded.

But by now it was clear that the other knight was dead.

After remounting his horse, Carados crossed the bridge, thinking he might try to lodge at the castle just beyond the river. But out from the castle gates burst another huge knight in vermillion armor, with his lance levelled and his shield raised. As he rode towards Carados, he issued his challenge: Wicked, base knight, I will avenge your murder of my brother. I defy you, and I will kill you.

Carados now charged towards this second knight. Their horses kicked up so much dust that Carados could barely see his opponent. Each knight's lance shattered into pieces against the other's shield, and the force of the blows hurled both men to the ground. Nevertheless, they stood back up again quickly and drew their swords.

Carados lunged madly at his opponent, even though he was much smaller—this was his chance to die an honorable and glorious death. The battle was fierce, but ultimately the bigger knight was too clumsy and slow in his movements, and Carados was able to land a blow deep into his underbelly.

The other knight collapsed onto the ground and dropped his sword. Carados knelt down, removed his helmet, and asked if he yielded and sought mercy. But the man used his last breaths to curse Carados for murdering a second knight in one day. Enraged at this arrogance, Carados cut off his head.

Carados then stood back up, covered in dripping, fresh blood, his muscles sore and exhausted. He returned his sword to its scabbard, remounted his horse, and began to trot slowly down the road.

But now a throng of men and women on foot burst forth from the castle. They ran to Carados, hailing him as a hero for delivering them from the tyranny of the wicked vermillion knights. They begged him to rest at the castle and enjoy their hospitality.

Carados followed the crowd back into the castle. Although the fortress was unimpressive—a stable, a smithy, and a two-story squat tower—the castle's residents were enthusiastic hosts. They removed Carados' armor and weapons and led him to a heated bath where many servants attended to his needs. After washing, they dressed him in soft, warm clothes and served him wine, fresh bread, and hard cheese in the modest hall.

As he ate, he was joined by an elegant, but gaunt, old woman. She smiled tenderly at Carados and encouraged him to eat his full.

When he was finished, she ordered the servants to bring her daughters into the hall, both of whom were lovely, bashful maidens.

The old woman asked Carados if he had heard of their plight and ridden forth from Camelot to rescue them. She had tried to smuggle messengers to King Arthur's court to seek the aid of their liege lord, but she had not been sure if the riders had made it past the two wicked knights.

Carados replied that he had not received word of the troubles in this region, and he did not think the lady's messengers had reached Camelot. He had simply gone forth as a knight errant seeking adventure and sought to put an end to an arrogant knight's wicked custom of blocking passage on the bridge.

The old woman beamed. It is God's will, then, she said, that you came to us. Our prayers were answered. I have always taught my daughters that you must put your faith and trust in God, and that if you are a good and sincere Christian, with Christ Your Savior always close to your heart, He will come to your aid.

The two lovely daughters dutifully and solemnly nodded their heads.

Carados asked if she could tell him what had happened here, and what crimes the two vermillion knights had committed. The old woman told him the following tale:

Her husband had been a brave and noble knight who had fought valiantly in King Arthur's early campaigns. When Arthur had brought peace to the land, he had given this fortress, bridge, and the surrounding lands to her husband to hold as his vassal. They lived many happy years here together.

But the long peace had made them docile and weak. Her husband grew old, and his joints became stiff. While the garrison in the castle had originally numbered six knights, there had been nothing for them to do in this place, and so those knights had eventually trickled away to other lands to seek adventure.

Several months ago, two knights in vermillion armor, brothers, knocked at the castle gates seeking hospitality for the night. Suspecting nothing, the lady's husband welcomed them graciously and served them with the best of everything he had. He was overjoyed to speak with fellow knights again and quizzed them eagerly about their battles and arms and horses.

Later that evening, the two knights slipped into her husband's bed chamber; they strangled him in his sleep. Then they woke the lady of the castle and showed her the corpse. We are the lords of this fortress now, they said, and we want your daughters for our wives. We command you to write to King Arthur in Camelot that your husband died of a sudden illness and that we, as his sons-in-law, are his proper heirs.

The lady refused. She cursed them as murderers and traitors and swore that God would have His vengeance upon such heathen scum. Furious, the knights threw her and her daughters into a cell in the dungeon. But the servants stayed loyal and secretly brought food and water to the noble ladies and told them what was happening—how one knight had taken over the fortress and the other knight had taken over the guard tower on the far side of the bridge. They used the bridge to rob passersby, not just knights but any merchant or farmer who happened to be unfortunate enough to ride past.

They drove out the castle's confessor and forced the blacksmith at sword-point to melt down the golden vessels in the chapel, so that the wicked knights could steal the Church's riches for their own personal gain. The lady and her daughters prayed day and night to Jesus Christ and His Holy Virgin Mother for deliverance from their ordeal.

And now the old woman cracked her warm smile again: Then you came, my Lord, and now we are free once more. God be praised!

Carados raised his cup and repeated the toast: God be praised!

Later that evening, the servants played music and danced in the courtyard. The lady's daughters joined in, but Carados declined on account of his fatigue and his wounds.

Carados spent four days in the castle resting and healing.

When he was strong enough to bear his arms again, the lady of the castle pulled him aside to speak privately. She praised his extraordinary courage and valor and said she had not been blessed to see such a fine and handsome knight since her husband, may his soul rest in peace, had fought side by side with the young King Arthur.

He thanked her for her kind words and praised her constancy in defending her family's honor and keeping the Christian faith, no matter how sorely those wicked knights had tested her.

Do you like it here, Sir Carados, in this castle? The forests in this country are filled with excellent game. The lord of this castle always feasts well and reaps many gold coins selling the hides and salted meats he does not need for his own household.

Carados nodded and mumbled about how fine the hunting must be.

And my daughters, she continued, are they not lovely? They zealously guarded their virginity throughout this terrible time. They are pious, good Christians. They will make loyal wives and excellent mothers.

Carados made no response. This conversation had begun to make him uneasy.

After a painful silence, the lady of the castle pressed her case further: Even though they are too bashful and modest to say so, I can see, the way only a mother can, how powerful an impression you have made on my daughters. I am sure either one would be happy to be your bride. Should you marry one of them—and you may take your pick—this castle and these lands shall be yours. Your fortune shall be made.

Carados reflected: She is sure I will not refuse a beautiful virgin and rich hunting lands. Yet it would be no use—I must still honor my oath and in less than a year's time submit to the blow from the giant. My bride will be a widow before she knows it, and any child will be an orphan.

I came here, his thoughts continued, to die a glorious and heroic death, so I would be celebrated as a fine knight and my family could honor and cherish my memory.

But I am still alive.

Nor do I have any glory. Nobody in Logres knew of the plight of these people; their messengers never made it to Camelot. Death here would have been no better than being mauled by a wild boar.

Carados now desperately wished to get away from this wheedling woman and her petty matrimonial scheming. Still, he was a knight of King Arthur's court and he needed to maintain a certain courtesy and decorum, especially to ladies of high birth. So, he did his best to make his exit graceful:

Lady, you flatter me. But I am too base and lowborn for your daughters. I am a humble knight errant, without even a squire to water my horse. I could never presume to take your esteemed husband's place as lord of this castle. I am sure your daughters will wed more noble husbands than me—their grace and beauty and high birth are apparent for anyone to see. Alas, I must ride on alone and seek further adventures.

Carados stood up and began to walk away. The lady of the castle turned pale. She grabbed the sleeve of his hauberk and pulled him back towards her.

Sir Carados, she said, you speak very foolishly. While I admit I do not know your lineage—although I suspect it to be far nobler than you say—your deeds have shown that you have the nobility of character to merit marrying a daughter of mine and ruling over this castle and fiefdom. You can sleep the rest of your nights on my soft sheets, next to a beautiful, smiling lady who will love you and bear you many sons. Surely that is better than riding alone after thieves and brigands in the woods. Stay here, and you can provide guidance and protection to the people of this fortress. They are good Christians, and they deserve a good Christian lord, young and strong, to watch over them and keep them safe.

Carados felt his patience wearing thin. He had freed her and slaughtered her enemies, even though it would win him no renown. Why couldn't she be satisfied with that stroke of good luck? If he had chosen to ride in a different direction, she would still be rotting away in her dungeon cell.

I am sorry, my Lady, he said, I must go.

But what will happen if another wicked knight comes to our gates and tries to take my daughters by force? They will be forever shamed. Please, stay, at least until another good Christian knight comes along who will agree to be our protector.

Carados firmly pulled her hand from his sleeve. I promise, my Lady, that I will send word immediately to King Arthur to send knights to garrison this fortress. I am sure His Majesty recalls well the many brave services your husband performed for him, and will no doubt send excellent men to your aid.

You will do that? she asked. Promise me, swear to me, please, I beg you.

Yes, of course, I promise, I swear.

And with that, Carados left the old woman, mounted his steed, and rode off through the gates, following the path back into the forest.

But he never sent word to Camelot of the small castle's plight, nor did he ever bother to inquire what became of the widow and her beautiful daughters.

IV. The Sorceress in the Tower

SIR CARADOS RODE through the forest until he eventually heard sounds in the distance of men shouting and metal banging. Following their direction, he came upon a wide meadow; in the middle sat a red marble tower surrounded by a moat and a thick stone wall. Massed around the outer wall were several knights, perhaps half a dozen in all. Carados rode up to the knight who appeared to be their leader and asked who lived in the tower and why they were attacking it.

A sorceress, a mistress of the Devil, lives there, he replied. She tormented the honest people of this country until we drove her back into her fortress. She is watching us from those high windows. We shall rid this land of her, in the name of King Arthur and the Holy Church.

What terrible deeds had she done? Carados asked. Perhaps, he mused to himself, this was the adventure he had been seeking: He could die fighting this witch and her demon lovers. That would be a glorious, perhaps even a saintly, death. Maybe the demons had assumed the shape of dragons—he could be another Saint George slaying the dragon, foul creature of Hell. His heart swelled with pride at his imagined glory.

What had she done? the other knight repeated. There had been strange happenings in the villages nearby. The peasants swore they saw giant horsemen riding in the woods at night, swinging huge axes—ghostly riders, who never spoke. If you saw one and were lucky, he would look right through you. But if he noticed you, he would slice off your head. Sometimes the riders themselves were headless and would try on the different heads of their victims as a sick jest.

Brave knights heard the tales told of these giants and they rode forth from Camelot, many famous men, Lancelot and Gawain and Gaheriet and Perceval, even Galahad, greatest of all knights. But when they arrived here, the giant riders were nowhere to be seen. The knights of the Round Table cursed the people in this country as superstitious fools.

The people, in their despair, turned away from King Arthur and sought help elsewhere. There are still pagans in these lands who deny the One True God and His Son begotten of the Holy Virgin. These wicked souls said the giant riders were Woden and Thor, angry at their worshippers for abandoning them in favor of the Church.

So, they started praying to Woden again, built him an altar and sacrificed goats and chickens. But when the heathens rushed to greet the giants at night, sure of their gods' blessing and mercy, the giants still cut off their heads all the same.

Yet then a miracle occurred, God be praised. A young monk was passing through. He begged a meal from a farmer, a good Christian man whose faith had never wavered. The farmer told the monk all about the giant riders in the night. The monk shuddered at these ungodly portents and prayed that night for guidance.

As the monk later revealed, he was gifted by God with a vision. The soul of a holy hermit who had lived in these parts, and whose bones are now kept in the local church as sacred relics, came to him in a dream. The hermit said these giant riders would reveal their secrets if a man of true faith approached them holding the holy cross and reciting a special prayer, which he imparted. This incantation was neither in Latin nor the common tongue, but something much older, an ancient language that sounds like metal daggers scraping against each other.

The next morning the monk summoned the people together and told them of his vision. He ordered them to assemble again at twilight in the church, each one carrying a cross in his hand or around his neck.

When the crowd had gathered at sunset, the monk sang mass for them and gave each one holy communion.

After night had fallen, the monk led the people into the woods. He told them not to fear, but to trust in God and His Son Jesus Christ and the Holy Virgin Mother. When a giant rider approached them, flashing his wolf-like teeth and swinging his axe, each man raised his cross high into the air.

The giant stopped dead in his tracks.

Then the monk strode right up to him, grabbed his horse's bridle, and spoke the strange invocation in the ancient, foreign tongue. The giant immediately dropped his axe, which vanished into smoke.

Spirit, the monk asked, why do you ride here and terrorize these good Christian people?

The ghoul responded calmly and clearly: Because I was summoned.

And who summoned you from the sulfur pits of Hell?

She summoned me.

And who is she?

I do not know her name. But I am bound to her service.

Can you take me to her?

And with that, the monk released his grip on the bridle. The spirit nodded silently and trotted slowly away. The monk and the others followed him.

The giant led them to the walls surrounding this tower. He pointed to the top window—the one right up there, you see—where a bright light illuminated a tall, red-headed woman being taken from behind by a man with goats' legs and horns and flaming red eyes.

Then the giant dismounted from his horse, which, like his axe, now vanished into smoke. He jumped over the outer wall of the fortress and disappeared into the night.

Meanwhile, the woman in the tower window smiled down at the crowd and made lewd gestures to show how fond she was of her demon lover—the vile witch had no shame whatsoever. Sickened and enraged, the people began to scale the walls. But every time they reached the top, they would suddenly find themselves back at the bottom.

The next morning the monk sent a messenger to the bishop to relate these marvels, just as I have told them to you. The good bishop, alarmed at these unchristian activities, dispatched us here. We have been laying siege to this tower, but we cannot break through the walls. The sorceress taunts us from her high window and tries to lure and tempt us away from our true faith with disgusting displays of her flesh, but we are steadfast, all praise be to Our Lord Jesus Christ for giving us the strength to resist her blandishments.

Carados was intrigued by this tale. He wondered if the giant returning to Camelot to kill him was the same as one of the giants who had haunted these woods. Or maybe they were kindred ghouls. Perhaps the sorceress in the tower knew how to command such fiends and could save him from his fate?

But for now, he pledged himself to assist the other knights in the siege.

For three days and nights, Carados tried to breach the walls, or at least to weaken them somehow, but to no avail. When he attempted to scale the walls, he too would find himself transported back to the ground as soon as he had reached the top.

Then on the third night, as midnight approached, sleep suddenly overwhelmed him. A soft, feminine voice called out to him; he recognized it vaguely.

The voice said: I can help you, Sir Carados. I can save you from your fate. But you must promise to heed my words.

In his dream, Carados answered her: Yes, of course, I promise.

When you wake, the voice continued, you will be inside my tower.

He then fell into a deep, dreamless slumber.

When Carados awoke, he found himself inside a spacious, but windowless, room lit by a chandelier hanging above his head. He did not know how long he had slept, the time of day, or how he had arrived at this place.

He had been lying on a hard marble floor. He stood up gingerly; his stiff joints and bones ached. He felt around his body and was reassured to discover that he remained fully armed.

In the middle of the room was a table piled high with food and drink. There was one chair by the table, with a note on it. Carados walked over and picked it up. The handwriting was lovely—large and graceful—and the parchment was perfumed with strong feminine, floral scents.

The note read: To my dear lord Sir Carados, I graciously welcome you as my esteemed guest. Eat and drink your fill. When you are ready, I will have you brought to me.

There was no signature.

Carados was uneasy but saw no obvious means of escape. Nevertheless, as he was feeling quite hungry, he decided to do what he could under the circumstances and sat down to eat and drink. To his happy surprise, the food turned out to be marvelous.

When he had eaten his full, he shouted at the ceiling: I am finished with my meal. I demand to be brought to my host, just as her note promised.

As if in response to his request, a door opened, even though Carados had been certain that there were no doors to this room. A very short, very elegant thin old man entered, bowed, and signaled to Carados to follow him.

They walked silently together up a winding staircase until they reached a landing with tall bay windows. Carados now saw it was nighttime and the moon was bright and full.

The old man motioned for Carados to follow him into another room.

In the middle of this room was an immense bed surrounded by thick red curtains. The old man walked over to the bed, disappeared into the folds of the curtains, and then out emerged a tall, elegantly dressed red-haired woman.

Carados recognized her at once: She was the woman from the phantom brothel, on that horrible drunken night in Camelot.

Sir Carados, she began, there is no cause for you to be so pale. I wish to help you. Won't you sit down, here on the bed?

But he stayed perfectly still, with his hand cradling the hilt of his sword.

She clasped her hands and forced a smile. Fine, Sir Carados, stand about and fondle your weapons all you like, much good they will do you here. But answer me this: What is it you desire most?

To die in glory for the good of the Crown of Logres and Christ My Savior, doing knightly deeds, he replied.

I don't believe you, she replied. Would you truly wish to die if the giant were not going to return next Christmas to strike a blow at your head?

Carados did not answer.

There is no shame in being afraid, she continued. You alone were noble and brave enough to answer the giant's challenge. The famous knights of the Round Table showed themselves to be base cowards. But now you are trying to cheat the giant by dying first in some new and different adventure. That is not chivalrous. Your true adventure is to solve the riddle of the giant's challenge.

Carados looked down at the floor and sighed. But it is hopeless, he said. I have sworn to submit to his blow next Christmas festival.

You are a young fool. You see only the surface of things. But I can teach you to grasp the deeper truth. I have communed with the hidden gods who are older than your Christ, the spirits who twist and bend men's fates.

Who are you, lady?

I am Morgan le Fay, your lord Arthur's half-sister. I learned the secrets of sorcery and necromancy, of the enchantments of the fairies and the otherworld, from the lips of Merlin himself, before the Lady Viviane tricked and murdered him.

What must I do, Lady Morgan?

We must leave this place. It is draining my strength to keep my attackers at bay—I cannot aide you in your adventure if I must devote my efforts instead to the defense of this tower. Let us break free of them, and I will take you far away from here, to a place where I can teach you the wisdom that you need to learn.

But first, you must pledge your loyalty to me.

Without hesitating, Carados walked over to Lady Morgan, knelt down before her, swore an oath of fealty, and kissed the ruby ring on her left hand.

She bade him rise and led him back down the tower's stairs. When they reached the bottom, she brought him to a side door that exited into the fortress stables. There he found two horses saddled and readied to mount—a silver palfrey for Lady Morgan, and his own charger, with his lance and shield hanging from the saddle.

They rode to the moat. Morgan uttered an incantation, and a bridge appeared, which they quickly crossed. Upon reaching the walls, she tapped them lightly with the end of a long, painted fingernail and they opened just wide enough for the two riders to pass outside.

The besiegers now rode towards Carados and Morgan as they emerged from the fortress walls. Carados leveled his lance and prepared to meet the challenge. But before he spurred his horse Morgan blew a dusty powder into his eyes. Suddenly he was able to see in the night as easily as he could in the daytime—and no doubt much better than his adversaries, he thought, who appeared to be moving at a cautious trot.

Carados kicked his spurs hard into his charger's sides, and the beast took off at breakneck speed. He drove his lance deep into the side of the first besieger and knocked him to the ground, bleeding profusely and screaming in agony. The other knights began to panic—they spoke of how only a demon could move so quickly in the darkness.

Carados made another charge and came upon a knight from behind, driving his lance through the man's spine and into his heart, killing him instantly. The remaining besiegers now fled, screaming in terror.

Lady Morgan rode up next to Carados and squeezed his hand. Follow me, she said, we will not be able to rest for some time. And she led him further into the forest.

V. Otherworlds

THEY RODE FOR three days without break. Whenever Carados felt he was about to collapse from hunger, thirst, or lack of sleep, Morgan would take his hand and mumble an incantation, and his strength would be miraculously restored.

He saw her now for the first time in the bright sunlight. She was certainly not pretty. Her face was harsh, with subtle but unmistakable lines and wrinkles slithering up and down her skin; he felt there was something knotted and angry about her features, even when she strained hard to appear demure and yielding. But her figure was tall and lithe, and her red hair was thick and luxurious.

He was not sure whether to trust her. He had heard many whispers of the foul cunning and black magic of King Arthur's half-sister Morgan. But then again, he mused, what was he chancing? His death was not only ordained, but precisely scheduled. No one else had offered to help him out of his predicament—certainly not Arthur or his knights.

Morgan eventually led him to an isolated clearing in the forest. In the center of the wide meadow was a hill, and atop the hill was a ruin. This building had been constructed from blue-veined marble, although it was now streaked with mud and grime, and its wide steps led to a portico with tall, rounded columns. At the back of this portico were two visibly rotting wooden doors.

As they approached closer, Carados made out a faded inscription in Latin above the doorway: Isis Welcomes All Who Are Weary.

Baffled by the inscription, he asked Morgan what this place was.

This is a temple that the Romans erected many years ago. When they abandoned Britain, the Romans left it here, tucked away in this forest. It is far from the old Roman forts, and I think they must have built it as a place of refuge or pilgrimage. It was a home for one of their goddesses, whom they brought with them to this island.

Do you know, Sir Carados, how long the Romans ruled Britain?

He admitted he did not. He knew they had slipped away just over three generations ago, and so only the very oldest of the old could remember a time when they were still around. To Carados, the Romans may as well have lived in the Garden of Eden, so distant did they seem.

For close to four hundred years the Romans ruled this land. Makes my brother Arthur's claim to glory seem rather slender, does it not?

Carados did not respond.

Come now, let's dismount, she continued. Tie the horses to those trees there, near the spring. They can drink their fill.

After Carados had taken care of the horses, Morgan led him up the marble steps of the temple and through the rotting wooden doors. Inside the air was so thick with dust that Carados fell to the ground in a painful fit of coughing.

Morgan laughed playfully at his distress. She walked around the dark, sooty room until she found and lit a large candle. Aided by the light, Carados now saw that the walls were decorated with paintings of the wonders of the sea: monsters and sirens, fish and birds, and wide blue skies resting easily above darker blue waters.

At the back of the room there was a raised dais, on which sat an altar and a marble statue of a woman. Her skin was dark and olive; her hair blue-black. Her almond-shaped eyes were kindly and compassionate.

Morgan took his hand and led him to a stone bench next to a wall.

Isn't it wondrous? she asked.

Yes, it is.

Just imagine, she continued, the wealth it must have taken to build this place. To buy and haul and cut the marble. To paint these walls, to chisel and paint the statue. And to do it all not in a king's great hall, but in some remote forest clearing. The Romans did not build this secluded temple to flaunt their riches or to intimidate their enemies. No, this was a melancholy reminder of their faraway homes—a balm for their loneliness in Britain.

We will remain here, Sir Carados, until you have learned what you must learn from me. In the back of the building, behind the altar, are the rooms where the temple attendants once slept. I have stored food and wine there, as I enjoy visiting this place from time to time. Let us eat and then rest.

She then led him into a narrow back room, where she lit another candle. Carados saw three stone slabs there covered with straw. From a corner, Morgan brought forth a barrel of wine and some bread and salted meats.

After eating and drinking his fill, Carados collapsed upon the straw bedding and slept for a long time.

When he awoke, he nibbled on a bit of bread and wandered back again to the front of the temple. There he found Morgan standing quietly and respectfully before the statue of the goddess. Sunlight streamed in from the half-opened doorway, reflecting with harsh brightness on her disheveled, loose red hair.

Without moving her eyes from the statue, she asked: Sir Carados, do you come from a noble family? With lands, titles, vassals?

Yes, I do, my Lady, although I have not slept in my father's castle in many weeks.

She nodded gravely, before asking another question: Have your noble forbearers endowed monasteries?

Yes, my Lady, we have endowed many holy places on our lands.

And your parents and grandparents and great-grandparents, did they spend lavishly on these monuments to the Christian faith? Did they build their cloisters and chapels to endure forevermore?

Of course. To say otherwise would be a terrible slander on their memory.

Look at this statue, she said. The man who endowed it was no doubt like your noble forefathers—wealthy, highborn, piously devoted to his goddess. He wanted to build her a temple to last forevermore, to comfort and soothe pilgrims and wanderers far into the distant mists of future times.

But now it is a forgotten ruin. In the coming years, lowborn, thieving men will stumble upon this temple, and they will seize and loot its riches. You are seeing this shrine in its last, fleeting days of beauty.

And the man who endowed this holy place? No one remembers his name. He might have led a life distinguished by honor and virtue. Or he might have been a criminal and a liar. Whatever he was, he is long forgotten, a pile of rotting dust and bones buried who knows where on some patch of land that the old Romans once ruled.

So, what lasting honor was there in building this beautiful place? There was none. The Roman lord, whomever he was, may as well have spent his gold on wine and whores.

And it will be the same with your family's abbeys and churches: Soon enough they too will be abandoned and forgotten and quietly looted of their riches on moonless, cloudy nights. And no one will care who endowed them or why.

Carados replied harshly, his voice trembling with disgust and rage: The knights who were laying siege to your tower were right, you are the Devil's mistress. Of course *this* place will fall, it is a shrine to pagan lies and idols. But churches, where God's truth is openly proclaimed and celebrated, will live on forevermore. The truth endures, wickedness and falseness do not.

He walked off and began to regather his arms.

Don't leave yet, she said. I still have not taught you how to avoid death at the giant's hands. If you leave now, you are sure to die when he returns your axe stroke at the next Christmas festival.

Carados stopped what he was doing and put his scabbard down. Fine, he said, then tell me straightaway what I need to know and do not try again to tempt me away from my Christian faith.

Morgan nodded. Let us sit on the bench over there again, in the corner. Listen well to the tale of how I acquired what wisdom I have.

After they had sat down, she began:

I was born in Cornwall, in Tintagel Castle. My father, Duke Gorlois, died when I was a little girl. He was a kind man. He would walk with me on the rocky shore, and we would collect seashells together. He would tell me to put them next to my ear. But when I would hear that terrible moaning sound that seashells make, I would drop them in terror. He would then kneel down, so that our eyes were level, and tell me not to be afraid. What you hear, Morgan, he would say to me, is the singing of the fairies—the shells captured their pretty song and held onto it tightly, saving it for a beautiful girl like you to hear. Then he would pick me up and carry me back to his horse, and we would ride home to the castle.

One day he and my mother, the Lady Igraine, rode off to a festival at the court of the King of Logres, Uther Pendragon. Uther had just vanquished the usurper Vortigern, and he had invited all his barons to celebrate with him.

I was sad to be left at home with my governess. I stared out at the sea from my bedroom window, and looked for fairies taking a swim—maybe I could convince one of them to take me to where my father had gone. My older sister Morgause laughed at me. What a crybaby you are, she would say, father is an important man, and he must perform his duties at court. If you were older and better mannered, you would understand these things. I would get angry at Morgause's haughtiness and throw my clothes and pillows at her head and scream and cry. My governess would then barge in and punish me for being such a wild animal—those were her words, I think, such a wild animal—and Morgause would watch, smiling that smug, arrogant smile of hers.

Eventually my mother returned home, but without my father and strangely surrounded by many knights, more than I had ever seen before in one place. They hauled barrels of wine and crates of food inside the walls and then barricaded the castle gates. I was told that under no circumstances could I leave the fortress. After I tried once to sneak out to the seashore, I was locked in my bedroom high up in the keep. My governess was ordered to stay with me at all times, even to sleep in my bed with me, which only made her more inclined to scold me—I suppose this was how she relieved the tedium.

A guard was posted outside my door. My mother told me that if bad men should break into the castle, the guard would protect me and make sure I escaped to somewhere safe.

But why would bad men come here? I asked. And where is father? And why am I not allowed anymore to go to the sea and hear the fairy songs?

She told me I was too young to understand—she sounded just like Morgause—but that father had to be away right now so he could protect us from wicked men who want to hurt your mother.

But what wicked men? I asked. And why do they want to hurt you, mother?

But nobody would explain it to me.

Weeks went by. I grew melancholy. I ate little, spoke less, and prayed constantly for my father to come home. I was sure that everything would be better once he was home: I would go to the sea again, the hulking knights would go away, and my mother would stop crying—she was even sadder than me. She kept cursing her sinfulness and her vanity, saying she was to blame for everyone's suffering.

And then it finally happened, or at least so I naively believed at the time: Father came home, riding through the gates at twilight. God had heard my prayers and taken pity on me. Mother was so happy, she threw her arms around his neck and kissed him on each part of his face. I ran up and pulled on his sleeve and asked him to take me to the sea, so we could collect shells again and listen to fairy songs. He said, not right now, little one, and then he turned away from me. He did not seem to care about me one whit, which was not like him. I should have known then that something rotten was afoot, but sad little girls whose hearts break with longing for their fathers do not make wise judgments.

Still, I went to bed that night trembling with joy, and dreamt of the adventures I was going to have again with my father as we collected shells and watched the birds and tried to meet the fairies.

But when I woke the next morning, father was already gone.

And then I was told later that day that he had been killed in battle. I was so angry at my mother, because she had selfishly kept him all to herself on that one last night, and she had not let me say goodbye or get one last kiss on the cheek. I hated her, I cursed her, I kicked her, and I punched her. She, however, seemed not to be sad or angry, but confused and frightened. She shivered and crossed herself repeatedly. At the time, I did not understand, but later I would.

The next thing I learned was that my widowed mother was going to marry King Uther Pendragon. We were leaving Tintagel Castle and moving to his palace in Camelot. Mother was not happy, though, and she often sat for hours in the windows of our old castle, staring silently out towards the sea. I asked her why she was sad, but she would not tell me. I was now a princess of Logres, she explained, and I needed to forget the past and concentrate on my new duties to my new father.

During these days, my slender mother grew a plump belly, and her seamstresses were constantly letting out her dresses to make more room for her bulging body. It occurred to me that she might be carrying a child, but no one would speak of it. I asked mother once about why her belly was bigger and whether there was a baby in it, but she just sighed and ordered me to leave her presence.

When we came to Camelot, it was a cold and rainy day. The streets were empty, the shops were closed, and our servants and Uther's servants bickered over the baggage and the horses.

Mother, Morgause, and I were led into King Uther's great hall. There, we were approached by two fat, hairy, little men; one wore a light blue silk robe and the other a wrinkled linen tunic. I thought at first they were trolls coming to eat us, and I screamed. Mother struck me on the cheek and told me to behave. The little man in the silk robe with the black curly hair turned out to be King Uther Pendragon himself. The other one, who had a long grey beard and dried leaves tangled in his hair, that was the enchanter, Merlin. They both seemed very pleased with themselves. Mother, though, was clearly struggling to maintain her dignity and grace.

Mother and Uther exchanged coldly polite greetings before parting ways to prepare for the wedding. Morgause and I were handed over to the care of a kindly old nun, who showed us around the castle and introduced us to the other children living there. We played games until dinner and then fell asleep.

The wedding was a blur—I vaguely recall an immense church—and how awkward and tense Mother looked in her gown and veil towering above that little troll Uther. I think he had a sweaty eagerness in the expression on his face, but maybe I am imagining that detail.

In my first years at Camelot, I was happy. My new governess, the old nun, was gentle and a good teacher. I remember there was a carpenter who liked to carve toys for the children—he made me wooden seashells and fairies so I wouldn't be so homesick for Cornwall. I learned to read, to embroider, to sing, to play instruments.

Uther paid me no heed. Mother spent most of her time by herself, usually praying in her private chapel. When she was not praying, she would read about the lives of the saints. She especially loved the legend of Saint Catherine of Alexandria. When I once asked why, she told me that she admired the faith that had given Saint Catherine the strength to choose martyrdom and death over marrying the wicked pagan Emperor who had shamed her and slandered her faith. And then Mother burst into tears and told me to leave.

As I grew from a child into a woman, I finally learned why Mother was so melancholy. I do not recall who told me first— maybe it was an old servant or a malicious nobleman passing through—but whoever it was, the truth shattered the tranquility of my soul. I learned that it was the knights of my stepfather, Uther Pendragon, who had killed my father, after Uther had made war on my parents because Mother had refused to lie in his bed and break her marriage vows to Father.

I confronted my mother: How could you have married this man, I asked, who tried to shame you and who murdered your husband for protecting your honor? I called her a faithless, greedy whore. I said she cared more for her palaces and her silks than the oaths she had sworn to Father before God.

She struck me across the face, but I hit her right back—who was she to hold me in judgment? I was thirteen years old then and had grown strong; my blow sent her to the ground.

Morgan, she said, you do not understand, you are a child. I had no choice. The land needed peace. And I had to protect my daughters.

But I did not believe her excuses. I spent the rest of the day brooding, my anger burning hotter and hotter. And then, at dinner, I could bear it no more: I shouted at Uther that he was a murderer and a ravisher of honorable women and a disgusting sinner. Several attempts to hush me failed, and in the end, I was forcibly dragged by two knights back to my bedroom.

The next morning, I was informed by my governess that I was leaving for a convent, to complete my education. Two servants packed up my belongings and, by the time it was the hour of terce, I was in a carriage being driven away. The convent was far—Uther obviously did not want me near him—and it took us five days to arrive there.

I spent the next five years at this convent. Although the sisters were strict, they were also quite learned and taught me many things. In particular, I sought out the sister who was famous as a powerful healer. As she and I grew closer, she began to share secret knowledge with me, of the kind that the Church forbids. At first, these were enchantments to fight illnesses. But then she showed me stronger, blacker magic. We would sneak away at midnight to the caves in the nearby cliffs, and we would use necromancers' spells to summon spirits and demons.

I kept a secret journal where I carefully copied out these spells in a cipher of my own devising. When I was summoned back to

Uther's court at the age of eighteen—for it was time for me to be married off—I brought this journal home with me.

Once back in Camelot, I sought to continue my studies. I knew that Merlin was the most learned man in matters of enchantment. I caught him staring at me during a festival and decided to press my advantage. I asked that ugly troll to escort me on long walks through the forest. I stifled my disgust—I never imagined a man could smell so awful, and he made these wheezing, panting noises when my dress brushed up against him—and I smiled at him and I stroked his cheek and his beard. Sometimes I would let my long hair graze against him. He would blush and shiver at these trifling favors, no doubt thinking his vile lecherous thoughts about my body. But he would also tell me whatever I wished to know about the magic arts.

Unfortunately, disgusting old men were my lot then. I was young and beautiful, but the young and beautiful men of the court, the handsome knights, kept their distance from me. I had obviously been marked as someone's virgin bride and there would be a harsh fate awaiting any other man who dared to be my lover.

Uther Pendragon had struck an alliance with Urien, King of Rheged. My flesh consecrated unto Urien as his bride was one of the terms of their treaty. When I was first told of my betrothal, I was happy: I would be Queen of Rheged, my sons would be kings, and my husband, while much older, was famous as a mighty warrior—he had led his kingdom's successful defense against the Saxon invaders.

Urien traveled to Camelot for the wedding. Even though I should have been wary—I was, after all, marrying a stranger whom my father's murderer had chosen for me—I still felt excited. There is something contagiously joyful about a wedding, the sun bursting through the stained glass in the church, the huge, smiling crowd hailing you as the lovely bride.

But when I beheld my groom, I was aghast. He was fat and bald. He walked with a cane, complaining loudly of the gout in his foot, and he smelled of garlic, ale, and sweat. After we spoke a few polite phrases to one another, I saw him exchange this glance with Uther—the look of a man who was pleased with the new horse he had just bought.

Thankfully, he drank to excess at the feast, and the gout had swollen his foot to the size of his large goblet, so he had no desire to share my bed on our wedding night. I spent that evening alone, in my room, weeping pitiably. I reflected that, in the years since my father had been killed, my life had been spent in the service of one filthy lecherous old man after another. I imagined lying each night in Urien's bed, his blubbery, hairy, sweaty belly rubbing on my slender chest, and I shuddered.

But then I tried to think of happier things. Perhaps I would be fond of the children I would bear. Or find a true friend among the ladies of the court. Or maybe even take a secret lover.

The morning after the wedding we set out for Rheged. When we arrived, I was relieved to learn that I had my own suite of apartments. My husband did not summon me to his bed for two more weeks, as he first waited for the attack of gout to pass. Eventually, though, I had to lie with him, and I did my duty as best as I could. He seemed to enjoy it, and there was some small comfort in feeling that I was easing the sufferings of his old age.

Children followed, all girls. But I did not care much for being a mother. I let their nurses and governesses tend to them. I could not stand the sound of a small child crying. I know these cries are supposed to arouse my compassion, but they made my head pound terribly and I fled. I can't tell you how I occupied myself in those early years of marriage—the days rolled together in a foggy haze, as if I was not fully awake.

And then Uther Pendragon died. I was overjoyed at the news. So was my husband: He began to scheme to claim the crown of Logres. After all, Uther had no natural-born son, so one of his sons-in-law should presumably be his heir.

But the cunning Merlin had already moved quickly to control the succession. A stone slab magically appeared in front of the steps of St. Stephen's Church in Camelot, with a sword stuck in it. Merlin, who no doubt conjured this trick, immediately proclaimed this wonder to be a sign from the Christian god that whoever could pull the sword from the stone was the rightful king. Why anyone would listen to Merlin, an unrepentant pagan who prayed to demons in the forest, was beyond my ken. But the common people and the priests believed him. You know what happened next: Arthur alone was able to pull the sword from the stone.

While this charade of Merlin's impressed the bishop and the peasants, the barons were not so easily moved. My husband and the other lords said they would never follow a lowborn man, for that is what they thought Arthur was.

But Merlin was undaunted. He announced that he would prove Arthur to be the highest born man in all of Britain, and he convened a great assembly for that very purpose. I was there, with my husband, Urien.

Merlin requested that my mother, the widowed Queen Igraine, stand before the assembly and answer his questions.

And then the filthy little wizard revealed the horrible truth about the last night that I had thought I had seen my father alive: Merlin had used his magic to make Uther appear in the guise of my father, so that my mother would be tricked by the illusion into permitting him to enter the castle gates, lying with him and sating his lust. The issue of that night of lies and treachery was Arthur, who had been taken away at birth by Merlin to be raised in secret and was now revealed to be the natural born son of King Uther Pendragon and Lady Igraine.

Now I, at last, understood everything—my mother's mysteriously swelling belly in the months before we came to Camelot for her marriage to Uther, and her tears, and her guilt.

Arthur was thus the rightful king of Logres. My mother fled in shame, and I never saw her again. I was told she traveled to a convent, far away somewhere in Ireland, where she took the veil under a false name. I was so disgusted by all of them—Uther, Arthur, Merlin—their plotting and their trickery, acting as if my mother was a filthy whore in a brothel.

And my husband was no better. I begged him to refuse his allegiance to Arthur. I told him to rebel, as my father had done. But Urien laughed at me. Your father was killed, he said, and while the lance was piercing his belly, Uther was using Merlin's sorcery to mount your mother from behind.

Urien swore his oath of allegiance with a smile—they all did. They toasted Merlin. They actually admired his conduct—they thought it was funny. I attended the feast held after Arthur's coronation, and the barons, my husband included, spent the evening trading lewd jokes about how Uther must have been so amused to outwit my mother and her honorable resistance to his lusts.

I feigned illness on the journey home, so I could avoid speaking to anyone. I prayed for a quick death or some other deliverance from the wickedness around me. And my prayers were answered—in a way. On my first night back in Rheged, at the midnight hour, a man appeared to me, wearing a silver robe that glowed in the moonlight. He was young and handsome, in a soft, feminine way. He said he had heard my prayers and wished to help me.

I asked if he was an angel from God.

No, he said, I am not from the host of the Christian god. I come to you from the older spirits, whom you once served, before your marriage. I want to help you, but you must return to the old ways of the forests again.

I swore I would do so.

That pleases me, he said, and soon you will be sent a redeemer. He will satisfy your yearnings.

I returned to the old ways, just as I had promised. I wandered deep into the woods and performed the ancient, secret rites of these lands. I engaged once more in necromancy and sorcery. When I began to question whether it was all for naught—perhaps the lovely silver man was an apparition sent by Merlin to trick me into who knows what shameful conduct—I then experienced the one true miracle of my life: love.

He came to the court in Rheged from Brittany. His name was Sir Accolon. He was the youngest son of a noble lord, with no chance to inherit, but he had become a distinguished knight. He offered his services to King Urien, who gladly welcomed him, and armed him, and gave him a bed in our keep.

Everything now changed. The court in Rheged was an assembly of round-bellied, old drunkards boasting of their pitifully few, endlessly repeated, trivial exploits from long ago. They enjoyed whiling away their days hunting puny, helpless animals—like hares. They would ride around the woods, guzzling ale, following their dogs about, and instead of felling dangerous boars, or even a deer, they would return with puffy, red faces and a couple of dead little rabbits.

But Accolon did not drink or hunt. He was tall and beautiful—he had such dark blue eyes, like the summer sky before a storm. And he was so graceful when he rode his horse and drilled with his weapons in the open meadows.

All the ladies of the court fell in love with him. But they were no match for me. Years of ale and rabbit stew with their fat, lazy husbands had turned them into ugly, puffy creatures reeking of onions and sweat. Whereas I had not only retained my natural beauty, but I was also able to use sorcery to enhance my charms.

Soon we were stealing away together in the night, riding through the forest. We took shelter from a sudden cloudburst in the ruins of an old Roman fort and unburdened our hearts to each other. We embraced tenderly. He expressed outrage at the wrongs that had been visited upon me and my mother. He swore he would protect me and keep me safe.

I should have been satisfied with that: a beautiful, kind lover who would defend me from harm. As Urien was neither a jealous nor an observant man, we could have dallied together in bliss forever.

But having seen what a good, honorable man Accolon was, I burned with ever greater rage that my half-brother Arthur ruled Logres and that my idiot oaf of a husband ruled Rheged. Accolon would make a far greater, and a far more just, king than either of them. He could start a new royal line, free from the taint of Uther and Merlin's crimes. And I could be his queen and bear his sons.

I spoke to my lover about my dreams. I urged him to take up arms and rebel, promising him the aid of all my magic and cunning. But Accolon recoiled in horror: He had sworn an oath of allegiance to Urien, before God and upon sacred relics, and Urien in turn had sworn an oath of fealty to Arthur. He insisted that to attack either man would be treason and betrayal.

Nevertheless, I refused to accept that Logres was fated to be ruled by base and wicked men. I invited Arthur to visit Urien's castle in Rheged. As I had hoped, he brought his sword Excalibur. You have heard of its wonders, no doubt—another gift from Merlin, who had used powerful enchantments to threaten and injure an old fairy, the Lady of the Lake, until she handed it over. But I knew its true secret, which Merlin had revealed to me: While the sword is strong, true invincibility comes from the scabbard. As long as Arthur should wear that scabbard, no matter what blow is struck upon his body, he will not lose a drop of blood.

When Arthur arrived and dined with us, I mixed a special mulled wine for him and his knights, which sank them into the deepest of slumbers. While he slept his enchanted sleep, I crept into Arthur's room and stole the sword and the scabbard.

I took them to the ruins of the Roman fort in the forest. Under the bright moonlight, I burned incense and recited incantations to summon Vulcan, a god of the old Romans. When the Romans abandoned their old gods for the Christian faith, the spirits of those gods had been left to roam the Earth, homeless and despairing, but still quite potent.

Vulcan was no tall, pretty Jesus with his long face straining toward Heaven. He was short and ugly with a limp and a tangled beard, and soot covered him from head to toe. He had been reduced to eking out a meager existence as a smith of magical arms and jewels. That night, I asked him to make me an exact replica of Excalibur and its scabbard, so that no human eye could tell the difference, but the copy would nevertheless lack the powers of fairy enchantment.

Vulcan demanded to know how I would pay him. I offered him gold, but he laughed—what was gold to an immortal god? I offered to bring him sacrifices but balked when he demanded a public festival in his honor—we are now, after all, good Christian people.

From the way he leered at me, I quickly realized what payment he actually demanded—the disgusting swarthy demon. Repulsed as I was, I knew there was no other way to achieve my aims, which were for the greater good of all the people of Britain. So, I gave myself to him, and he in turn did the magical smithwork that I needed.

The next morning, while everyone else was still under the spell of my wine, I placed the false Excalibur and its scabbard at Arthur's side, and hid the real enchanted weapon in my rooms.

After our guests had finally woken, heard Mass, and ate breakfast, I suggested to Accolon that he escort Urien and Arthur on a ride through the forest. The three men heartily agreed, as I knew they would.

I secretly followed them into the woods.

When they reached the river, I conjured a boat to appear on the waters floating towards them. The crew were phantoms, restless souls of beautiful women who had been murdered in those lands by cruel men.

Once he had caught sight of the beautiful maidens, Arthur insisted that the three of them board the ship. After they had tied their horses to nearby trees and entered the boat, they reclined on soft couches beneath the deck as the sprits poured wine down their throats, and they sailed far away down the river.

The wine was a sleeping potion, and the three men quickly succumbed to its power. At my direction, the ghostly maidens carried each man to a different place. Urien was returned to his bed in Rheged. Arthur and Accolon, however, were taken elsewhere.

What I desired was for Accolon to defeat and kill Arthur in battle. The barons and the knights of Logres believed my brother to be invincible—more lies that Merlin had weaved around Arthur. Merlin had used tricks and sorcery to aid Arthur in his early battles, creating the false impression that Arthur was more than a mere man. I knew that if Accolon could slay my brother in combat, then Arthur's supporters would grovel before him.

I had learned that two brothers were disputing their father's inheritance and had agreed to settle their disagreement in a trial by combat. I had used witchcraft to inflict severe injuries on the inner thighs of each brother, so that they could not ride a horse or hold a lance steady. Thus, they would each need a champion for the trial by combat. I compelled the spirits to transport Accolon to one brother and King Arthur to the other. The demands of honor, and the threat of imprisonment, or worse, by their new hosts, compelled both Arthur and Accolon to agree to fight on behalf of the brother into whose clutches I had delivered him.

The night before the battle I visited Accolon in secret. He asked me how I had found him, but I reminded him that I possessed a vast knowledge of the dark arts. We kissed and embraced, and I swore my eternal love to him. I gave him the true Excalibur and scabbard. I did not tell him these were Arthur's weapons, but I said they were enchanted; if he used them in the next day's battle, he would not be defeated. He thanked me and I departed.

The next day, at the hour of prime, the two champions met in battle. However, since they both carried new shields and their helmets concealed their faces, neither man could know who his opponent was.

They charged hard with their lances and unhorsed each other. After lying stunned on the ground for a few minutes, each man got up, drew his sword, and commenced fighting on foot. Accolon had the upper hand, because, while Arthur bled from his wounds, Accolon did not—the scabbard's magic was working to deliver him a great victory.

But then suddenly the Lady of the Lake appeared, riding a white unicorn and wearing a blindingly bright white dress. She rode up to Arthur and whispered something in his ear. Everyone, including Accolon, stood in dumbfounded silence watching her.

Before Accolon could recover himself, Arthur lunged at him and cut the scabbard from his belt. Arthur now put the true, magical scabbard on his belt and went on the attack. With the enchanted weapon back in Arthur's hands, he quickly knocked Accolon down with so many blows that my beloved could no longer stand up.

Arthur removed his adversary's helmet and recognized Accolon immediately. Traitor, he screamed, you are forsworn to King Urien and to me.

Now realizing that he had been fighting King Arthur, Accolon, with his dying breaths, begged forgiveness, swore he had not known that he had been battling his liege lord to whom he owed fealty, and cursed me and my treachery. He told Arthur, in the hearing of all assembled there, how I used dark magic and worshipped demons, how I had seduced him and tried to rouse him to rebellion, and finally how I had come to him the night before and given him the enchanted scabbard and sword.

I fled from the spot where I had been discreetly watching the battle and rode deep into the forest. After a few days in hiding, I ventured forth again. To avoid being recognized, I cast a spell to make myself appear in the guise of a leprous old woman. Speaking to passersby on the road, I learned that I had been condemned as a traitor, that my husband had sued for divorce on the grounds of adultery, and that I had been banished forever from the courts of both Logres and Rheged.

In my wanderings, I chanced upon a wide meadow with an abandoned Roman fort—crumbling walls, shallow moat, modest tower. Using various enchantments, I summoned old spirits, older even than the Romans. They rebuilt the tower and its fortifications and sealed it with a spell. That is the place where you found me under siege.

I sat in my tower, alone, and reflected upon my fate. I had seen wickedness triumph, again and again, and I had seen virtuous men—my father, my lover Accolon—crushed underfoot. I thought of how my father had struggled so valiantly against Uther to protect my mother's honor and good name. But my father had been cut down, and Uther Pendragon took possession of my mother anyway and sired Arthur upon her. That wretched wizard who had enabled Uther to indulge his lusts, that filthy imp Merlin, then ensured the succession of Arthur by tearing from my mother the last shreds of dignity and pride she had left. Now my fate was following a similar path: I had tried to overthrow the corrupt lords who rule these lands and install a man of virtue as king, but the results of my efforts were that my lover was dead, I was cast out as a traitor and a whore, and the same wicked men still sit comfortably upon the same gilded thrones, doing as they please.

It is all illusion and lies, I finally realized. Honor, shame, chivalry, fealty—nonsense words, which men toss about in the wind to justify their crimes. There was no purpose in fighting against Arthur or Urien or Merlin or any of the rest of them. The only thing left to me was my own pleasure, the rest of it be damned.

So, I resolved to remain in my tower. I used my secret arts to summon whatever I desired—images of sweeping vistas, demons in the guise of beautiful and witty lovers who were eager to amuse me, delicacies to eat the likes of which you cannot imagine.

And the old heavy burdens floated off my heart.

But then, more wicked men came and laid siege to me, spoiling my paradise. For even though I am learned in the ways of sorcery, it still takes effort and strength to harness my powers, and now that effort and that strength had to be spent in keeping the rabble of smug, raging knights from knocking my walls down.

With your arrival, though, I saw how we could both be happy. Beneath this temple is a passage to the Otherworld, the realm of the ancient fairies, where we can rejoice forever in each other's arms, in unending bliss.

Here is my counsel—the wisdom you have been seeking—for keeping your head attached to your neck: Abandon your stupid oath to the giant, and forget your qualms about honor and shame. What good is your honor to you if you are dead? And even if you somehow survive the giant's challenge, what then? There will be more adventures, and tournaments, and wars, and your luck will run out sooner or later, just like my father, just like Accolon; someday, your horse will slip in the mud and an enemy lance will run right through your heart.

Morgan now leaned over, grabbed the back of his head, and kissed him passionately. Carados yielded himself willingly. He had been mesmerized by the rhythms of her voice and moved by her tale. He was sure that she had finally given him the wisdom he needed—his oath was a false idol, and one he could readily smash with his fist. Eternal pleasure, delicacies to eat beyond the mortal imagination—that was what he should pursue, the hell with oaths and honor and chivalry. It was not as if King Arthur, or any of the other knights of the Round Table, had come to his aid.

Morgan rose and took his hand. He docilely followed her as she led him out of the temple, down its front steps, and around the hill. Beneath the temple, in what he had thought was a patch of tall grass, she uncovered a lavender-colored door. Morgan then uttered a series of strange words he did not understand, and the door opened.

On the other side of the door, Carados entered a palace, but it was far more splendid than any earthly palace. The building was fashioned entirely from green-veined white marble, and bright, vivid tapestries of lovely fairies and mischievous satyrs hung upon the walls. A distinguished old servant greeted them and escorted them to a great hall where they were served a sumptuous feast—Carados had never tasted such finely spiced, such perfectly cooked, food.

After they had eaten their full, the old servant reappeared to lead Carados and Morgan to their bed chamber. In the dim orange candlelight, Morgan led him through the thicket of heavy curtains around the canopied bed into the soft sheets and undulating mattress. The lovers embraced, coiled and uncoiled, and the burdens weighing upon Carados' heart melted away.

Many days seemed to pass in this manner—feasting and embracing and drinking sweet wine in the vast palace of the fairies—until Carados lost track of time and could not tell day from night, or week from week. Sometimes he wondered if the

Christmas festival was approaching, if perhaps he should consider leaving and honoring his oath to the giant. But then he put such thoughts out of his mind: He would not pointlessly sacrifice—no, sacrifice was the wrong, he would not toss into a rubbish heap— his life now that it had become so sweet with pleasure. He thought: Why must my joys ever end? In the world of knights and chivalry, I am doomed to die while the cowards who avoided the giant's challenge will live to a fat, happy dotage. Damn them all.

And then the unpleasant thoughts of the giant and the oath and the upcoming Christmas festival would fade away, like dark shadows driven out by the sunrise, and he would lose himself once more in drink and Morgan's honeyed, soft kisses.

VI. Shame and Dishonor

CARADOS WOKE WITH a start. He had no idea where he was; his back was stiff, and his fingers were buried in dirt and grass. The sun was painfully bright, forcing him to shield his eyes. With an effort, he sat up and looked around. He was in a forest somewhere, with no one else around. A deer darted by indifferently.

He stood up and tried to get his bearings. He had been in the fairy palace, in the soft bed … and then it was a blur. He did not remember how he had come to sleep in the woods, and there was no sign of the hill, the temple, or Morgan. Had it all been an illusion? For a moment, he was angry at himself for having been so naïve as to be tricked by a cunning sorceress. But then he reflected: Even if it had been an illusion, it was a pleasant one, and what had been the harm to him—too much fine wine and too many moist kisses?

He suddenly felt quite hungry, as if he had not eaten for days. Which was strange, because he clearly remembered stuffing himself to the brim the previous night with the most wonderful delicacies. He looked around for a weapon to hunt his breakfast but found none. His weapons and armor had disappeared, and he was, inexplicably, wearing wrinkled, smelly peasants' clothes.

With no better option, he began to walk. After a little while, he found a road cutting through the forest, which he followed to a village. He begged bread there from the sisters at a convent, which quelled his hunger. He asked the good nuns where he was and how to reach Camelot (where he reasoned he could acquire a new set of arms and a horse). They told him he was only a day's walk from Camelot and kindly gave him provisions for the trip.

When Carados saw Camelot's walls looming before him the next day, his heart quickened with joy. But by the time he had reached Camelot's gates, they had been locked for the night. Fearing the sentries would not recognize him in his ridiculous peasant garb, he went to sleep in the surrounding meadow, watching the stars overhead and whistling merrily. He dreamed of once more holding a sword in his hand.

The next morning, between the hours of prime and terce, Carados ambled through Camelot's gates alongside peasants pushing carts piled high with butter, cheese, and squawking geese. He looked around for someone he knew, but the streets were largely deserted.

He went to King Arthur's palace, but the doors were bolted shut.

He next turned his steps to the stables, which were almost completely empty; the only horses he found were scrawny, old, and weak. There were a few sullen servant boys about, grudgingly feeding half rotted oats to the feeble animals.

Carados grew worried. Perhaps Logres was under attack and Arthur had been compelled to marshal his forces. If his lord were in danger, Carados felt he should be in the battle too, armed and defending the kingdom—he would rightly be judged a treacherous coward if he idled away his time with women instead of being counted among the realm's champions.

He cursed Morgan le Fay under his breath. Her fine, clever words, about how nothing mattered but the flesh and its delights, had lost their power to enchant once he had become concerned that King Arthur was being challenged in battle—how could he have been so foolish as to lap up such nonsense.

He wandered some more, still encountering almost no one, until he at last found a tavern. Thinking that maybe there would be a knight or squire inside drinking ale, he went in. However, the room was empty and Carados was about to leave, but then the tavern keeper came over and urged him to stay. He could use the company, he said, and offered a mug of mead and a hunk of barley bread at no charge. Feeling hungry, Carados sat down and ate and drank.

Friend, where are you from? the tavern keeper asked.

Carados answered that he was a knight errant who had been robbed of his arms and his horse by a thieving whore.

The tavern keeper smiled. That will teach you to be too trusting of the ladies, he said, all smiles and kisses until you fall asleep, and then when you wake up, you are all alone with your purse empty and your possessions gone. Still, I am sure she gave more pleasure than the Christmas festival here. After the shame of it, everyone sulked away, their heads held low.

Carados said nothing but racked his brains to understand how so much time could have passed that it was already past Christmas.

You don't know, do you? the tavern keeper continued after a pause. She must have been something to keep you so distracted.

What happened at the Christmas festival? Carados asked.

The tavern keeper sighed wistfully, and then told the tale: King Arthur had returned at Christmastime to his hall in Camelot and summoned a magnificent court with all his famous knights in attendance. I could hardly keep up with their demands for ale, mead, wine, mutton, pork, bread, cheese—so much eating and drinking that my purse burst with coins, praise be to God.

All the lords and ladies were excited because a great marvel was expected. One year before a giant had strode into King

Arthur's hall and offered a challenge: A knight could take one swing of the axe at his neck then and there, with no resistance, so long as that knight would agree that the giant could return the blow a year later. Most knights knew better than to try this adventure—they had seen enough of trickery and sorcery to be wary of challenges like this—but one young knight accepted, swung the axe, and sliced the giant's head clean off. But then the giant picks up his head off the floor and walks away. So now, everyone wanted to see if the giant would return as he had promised and if the brave young knight would survive the reciprocal blow.

But the young knight, whatever his name, was not in Camelot. There was lots of speculation—maybe he was waiting for the giant to arrive first; maybe he was hiding or traveling incognito, biding his time for just the right moment to make himself known.

At the exact appointed time, the giant barges back into Arthur's hall, riding his huge horse and carrying his big axe. He demands satisfaction. He reminds His Majesty's court that he had meekly submitted to the knight's blow the previous Christmas. It is only fitting and courteous, he says, that the knight should now fulfill his oath and submit himself to the giant's reciprocal blow.

But this young knight is still nowhere to be found.

So, the giant says he will wait. He dismounts and sits himself down on the floor of King Arthur's hall with his big axe lying on the ground next to him.

But just the same, the young knight does not come forward to fulfill his oath.

And all the while the giant taunts His Majesty: So, this is how the knights of your court respect solemn oaths sworn on holy relics? This is how they show their courage and honor? Aren't you worried, oh great and mighty king, that the knights seated around you here may not have sincerely meant the oaths of fealty they each gave to you? After all, what worth was your knight's sworn oath to me?

King Arthur, and his knights, and the Queen, and her ladies, sat there silently, deeply shamed. They whispered fervent prayers to Christ in Heaven to speed the arrival of the young knight, but their prayers were in vain.

Three days the giant sat in King Arthur's hall, laughing and mocking, eating and drinking.

Finally, after three days, the giant left.

And that leave-taking was the worst of it. While the giant was sitting there, spewing insults and guzzling wine, there was still a chance—maybe the young knight would come and face the challenge, maybe the honor of Logres would be redeemed. But once the giant had left, it was hopeless: the young knight was forsworn.

As those who were there told it to me, after the giant had departed, the lords and knights and ladies sat in angry silence until Her Majesty Queen Guinevere at last rose to her feet and formally accused the young knight of treason. She asked if there was a champion for her cause in a trial by combat against the wicked oath-breaker. Sir Lancelot immediately agreed to ride forth and fight for the Queen's honor.

A date was set for the contest and messengers fanned out from Camelot across Logres and the neighboring lands to find the young knight and summon him to the battle.

But once more, no one could find him.

On the appointed day, Lancelot, shining in his white armor, rode forth to the meadow just beyond Camelot's walls. The whole court had assembled to watch the trial of the forsworn young knight.

But once again, he never came.

His Majesty King Arthur could no longer contain his wrath. He said that there was no reason to believe the young knight had been sick or wounded, and thus prevented from answering the summons to arms; if that had been the case, then surely one of the many messengers dispatched from Camelot would have learned of such extenuating circumstances. No, the young knight clearly had no excuse—he had broken his oath to the giant, an oath made upon holy relics, and then fled like a coward from the trial demanded by the Queen. King Arthur accordingly proclaimed judgment condemning the missing knight and decreed that any knight who should encounter the criminal, in any time or place, carry out immediately the royal sentence of death and bring the wretch's head on a spike back to Camelot.

Then they all scattered every which way. No one wanted to be in Camelot anymore—the shame of His Majesty's court was too much to bear.

So now here I am, sitting in my tavern, drinking alone. There is only despair in Camelot—if one of the king's knights is a traitor, swearing false oaths upon holy Christian relics, then who knows about the rest of them? Maybe there are other lords lurking about who would also break their oaths? Shame and suspicion spread like a loathsome disease in a brothel. Even the washerwomen now accuse each other of treachery.

And still nobody has laid eyes upon that young knight. But every champion of the Round Table is eager to find him and run the bastard through with the sharp iron tip of a good lance.

Why are you so pale, my good sir? Have some water. Will do you good, water and bread, plain and simple, just like the holy saints in the desert. There you go, that is better.

VII. Robber Baron

CARADOS SPENT THE rest of the day in Camelot doing his best not to be seen, hugging the shadows in the alleyways and keeping his hood down over his head. His thoughts had narrowed to a single point: the need to escape the vengeance of Arthur's knights and find a secure refuge.

As dusk approached, when the sentries would secure the city gates for the night, Carados slipped back outside Camelot into the countryside. Although he still had no horse or hauberk, he had managed to steal a sword, which had been left lying on the ground near a guard post, so he had at least some means of defending himself.

Carados walked quickly across the open meadow, careful however not to move so fast that he would draw the attention of the suspicious eyes keeping watch on the ramparts. His heart was heavy and cold with fear, and the stretch of open country seemed never to end.

At last, he reached the forest. By now, the sun had set, and a cloudy, moonless night had descended. Knowing he needed to make the most of the darkness, he dove into the densest patch of the woods, tripping over the many roots and branches that were concealed in the gloom.

Carados collapsed in exhaustion and fell asleep near dawn. When he awoke, his limbs stiff with pain, he found that he was near a lake with plentiful fish to catch. After he had eaten and drunk, he went deeper into the forest, moving steadily north.

He passed many days wandering in the thickets, far from the paved roads, drinking from dirty springs and eating whatever fish or rodents he could seize with his bare hands. Carados felt his hair grow wild and tangled, and his feet were covered in blisters and scabs.

His mind had gone largely blank, thinking only of where to find water, and how to catch and skin another rabbit. He often forgot why he had fled or what his life had been like as a knight. His worries melted away, and his soul found peace living like an animal in the forest.

But his bestial idyll ended when he again encountered his fellow man.

He had been resting by a lake when three men approached him. They were not impressive: short, wiry, twitching men, with narrow rat faces and darting paranoid eyes. They pounced upon Carados and demanded his money.

He looked up at their angry, greedy little faces and laughed.

This seemed only to enrage the robbers more. One of them grabbed Carados by his long hair and pulled him upright, while another drew a dagger and put it to his throat.

Again, they demanded Carados' money.

Acting on instincts buried deep within the recesses of his mind, Carados twisted his body quickly, broke the grip on his hair, pulled out his sword, and ran it through the belly of the man with the dagger.

The other two robbers stepped back.

Carados, for his part, felt an unexpected joy: He had sorely missed the excitement of killing other men. A sense of power surged in his veins, and, on a sudden giddy whim, he sliced off the head of his victim.

He looked back again at the other two men. He hoped that they would attack him and try to avenge their fallen comrade, so he would have an excuse to continue the fight and spill more blood.

But the other robbers did not attack, or even appear upset. They shrugged their shoulders, and one of them kicked his fallen comrade's decapitated head into the lake.

One of the robbers asked Carados to which band of forest thieves he had sworn allegiance.

Carados said he had sworn fealty to no man. He lived as he pleased and ate what he killed.

The robber replied: You should join our band. We don't dine on little trout from streams—we feast upon fat pigs roasted on spits and huge legs of mutton. We could use a swordsman like you.

And you could use our help. These woods are filled with desperate, starving men. One of these days someone will come along and cut your throat in your sleep. If you are part of our band, we can keep you safe.

Carados mulled the robber's proposition. While he enjoyed his freedom, he could not dispute the danger: Perhaps some desperate man would cut his throat in the night.

Or worse: One of King Arthur's knights would find him.

So Carados accepted the robber's offer and followed the two men through a series of tangled, narrow paths to a clearing in the woods. There he found a ruined hunting lodge, its doors barely still hanging onto their hinges and the wind whistling harshly through the cracks in the walls. Inside he met the other members of the band of thieves.

After hearing of Carados' skill with his sword, these men likewise shed no tears for their fallen comrade, but rather hailed Carados as their new champion. He indifferently repeated whatever oath of loyalty they recited in their mock pompous manner, and then dined with them—a rich meal of pork and herbs and ale, the best fare he had eaten in many nights.

Carados adapted easily to the life of a thief. He enjoyed lying in wait where the forest highways made narrow turns, and then pouncing upon unwary travelers. He robbed, beat, and occasionally killed all classes of society: peasants taking goods to market, merchants with thick purses, monks collecting alms, noble ladies on their way to secret trysts with knightly lovers.

No one in the ragtag group of robbers could match Carados' skill and agility with his sword, or his bodily strength. They quickly acknowledged him as their leader.

The only thing marring his happiness was the crumbling and decrepit hunting lodge where the band of rogues ate and slept. Not only was the building draughty and falling apart, but it had no defenses—no ramparts, no moat—and the rotting wooden beams could easily be set ablaze by attackers.

What they needed, he felt, was a fortified castle, on a strategic high ground overlooking and controlling key passes on the roads and highways.

So Carados ordered his followers to abandon the lodge and wander the countryside, sleeping in tents or old Roman forts. While his men cursed him on cold, rainy nights, he counseled patience: They would find a castle they could take, and make that their new home.

One day they chanced upon a modest castle perched upon a bluff overlooking a river. From that vantage point, the countryside for miles around was easily visible, including many roads.

Carados carefully surveyed the defenses: no moat, no sentry tower, and the outer walls full of cracks and moss. He saw no knights patrolling the area. Still, he was cautious: If there were well-equipped knights hidden inside the walls, then they would easily butcher his shabby band of thieves.

Carados directed the oldest member of their group, their cook, to approach the castle under the pretense of being a beggar, spend the night, and then report back. In the meantime, Carados and his men kept their distance under the forest's cover.

The next morning the cook returned to the robbers' camp and gave his report: He had entered the castle with a fake and exaggerated limp, crying for alms. He had been given food and a place to sleep in the stables.

He had asked the stable hands for the name of the lord who ruled the castle and whether there were strong knights protecting it.

The stable hands shook their heads and sighed loudly. Once, they explained, the lord of the castle had been a fearsome knight who had kept a garrison of ten other knights with him. But then word had come of Saxon raiders marauding in the area, stealing crops and violating the honor of the local women. The lord was furious and rode out with his knights to battle the Saxon riffraff.

But he never returned: The Saxons drove a pike through his heart. And even though the Saxons suffered heavy losses and were forced to retreat, only three knights came back alive to the castle. Each surviving knight then demanded the hand of the lord's widow in marriage and that his comrades swear fealty to him as lord. Having no other means to settle who should become the new lord of the fortress, they jousted. The strongest of the three knights so brutally unhorsed the other two that each broke his neck and died soon afterwards.

The widow was horrified. She refused to wed the victorious knight unless he did penance for the sin of murder and pledged himself to be a good Christian—no more tournaments or jousts or challenges to prove his superiority or defend his honor; she insisted he should only fight as necessary to keep innocent people safe from harm.

The knight was outraged and told the widow she would condemn him to a life of ridicule as a coward. She could have his protection and his love, he said, or he could ride away and pledge his sword in service elsewhere, where he could live without shame and disgrace.

But the widow would not relent, such was her fear of God, and so the knight rode off. She now lived in the castle alone with her aunt and her confessor. She had sent messengers to King Arthur's court, begging for a champion to come to her aid and to be a good Christian lord of her lands, but no hero had ridden forth.

To defend the castle, the servants had armed themselves with the fallen knights' weapons and stood guard at various places, but they could barely lift the heavy swords and lances, much less wield them. The stable hands were sure the castle would fall sooner or later, and they were plotting their escapes.

Carados smiled as if he had, at long last, found just the right wine to soothe his thirst. He ordered his men to rest and sleep that day, so they would be fresh in the evening for the assault on the castle.

Once darkness covered the sky, and no lights could be seen in the keep's windows, Carados launched his attack. His men easily broke the rusted lock on the gate and made for the palace. The castle's servants, who were posted as sentries, dropped their weapons and fled screaming in every direction.

Carados told his men to let the servants go. Finding the palace doors bolted shut, Carados went to the stables and fetched a horse. Picking up a heavy lance that a servant had dropped, Carados charged hard and fast at the wooden palace doors and smashed them to bits with the metal tip of his lance. He rode straight into the hall, shouting wildly, with his ecstatic, cheering men in tow.

But the lady of the castle was nowhere to be seen.

After a thorough search, they eventually found her, with her aunt and her confessor, in a small chapel grasping a statue of the Virgin Mary and begging for heavenly aid and deliverance.

Carados approached them and asked that the lady surrender. If she were to surrender, and agree to be his wife, he would let her and her companions live.

But they ignored him and continued their frantic prayers.

So Carados dragged them away from the Holy Virgin Mother's statue and placed himself directly over their kneeling, quivering bodies. He repeated his terms again.

But they still would not acknowledge or answer him.

Losing his patience, Carados grabbed the wimple of the younger looking of the two women, whom he assumed to be the lady of the castle and pulled her head up so that she was looking directly into his eyes.

Lady, he said, do you agree to surrender and become my wife, or do you choose to meet your beloved Virgin?

The lady of the castle finally stopped her wailing and stared, in grave silence, into Carados' eyes. Her glare felt uncomfortably heavy, but he steeled himself to wait for her response—this would be easier if she would wed him and thereby confer legitimacy upon his claim to the castle and the surrounding lands.

But then the lady of the castle at last gave her response to the invaders: a violent shriek as if the hounds of hell were tearing her flesh apart.

Enraged, Carados grabbed her throat and squeezed with every ounce of his strength until he felt her windpipe fracture in his fingers. Relieved to be rid of her screaming, he carelessly tossed her corpse aside.

Turning to the lady's elderly aunt, Carados again demanded surrender. But after she spat in his face, Carados unsheathed his sword and ran it through her gut. As she doubled over in pain, bleeding out rapidly upon the ground, he repeatedly kicked her head into the hard, jagged flagstones until his boots were covered with sticky, small fragments of her skull and brain.

The priest staggered back and crossed himself. He begged leave to give the two ladies a proper Christian burial at a nearby abbey. But Carados did not trust him: What if the priest were to send for a champion to avenge his mistress? So Carados grabbed the priest and drove his sword through the cleric's heart.

He ordered his men to burn the corpses and scatter the ashes in the dungeon.

The next day the band of thieves rounded up the servants who had gone into hiding or attempted to flee. They were granted clemency and protection in exchange for their oaths of fealty, which they quickly swore to their new lord.

With his followers' ranks now swelled by the castle's servants, Carados spent the next several weeks fortifying and securing the citadel, including digging a proper moat.

Once they were well-entrenched, Carados posted watchmen at key passes overlooking the roads passing below the castle. Should a defenseless traveler be spotted, a torch would be lit as a beacon. Carados would then arm himself and, accompanied by two or three men with axes, ride down to intercept the wayfarer on the road. On pain of death, he would demand an exorbitant highway toll—in the name of his right as lord of those lands to exact whatever taxation he deemed fitting and appropriate.

By despoiling many travelers in this way, Carados and his band grew rich. They drank prodigiously and took coarse peasant mistresses, whom they showered with silks and jewels in exchange for their favors. The lord of the castle, himself, kept three such mistresses and sired several bastards.

With his soul happily occupied by violence, greed, and debauchery, Carados rarely thought of the noble, courtly world of his youth. Nevertheless, from time to time he would recall the wisdom of the sorceress Morgan le Fay, which always resonated in his heart: Nothing mattered in this world but seizing pleasure, as virtue is impotent and courtliness but an opaque veil spread over festering corruption.

VIII. The Quest for the Holy Grail

THE NIGHT WAS miserable—the bitterly cold wind slithered and twisted into every room, and from there into the marrow of Carados' bones, and the incessant noise of the rain and the wind pounded upon his ears. His mistresses buried themselves in shawls and blankets and shivered in corners like sickly rats. To top it all off, his food was bland and stale, and the wine tasted sour.

And then there was a loud banging at the castle gates. Carados dispatched a guard to see who it was. His sentry reported back that there was a knight, riding alone, who sought shelter from the storm and a place to rest until the morning.

Carados did not like the idea of an unfamiliar knight roaming his lands. He mulled the matter briefly. Trying to kill the stranger immediately was risky, as Carados did not know how strong he was, or how well-armed. Better to bring him in, disarm him, and ply him with wine and questions.

So, the knight was warmly welcomed into the castle, and disarmed by gracious servants who dressed him in a fine burgundy mantle. He was shown into the hall, where Carados offered him strong wine and a thick venison stew.

The knight ate and drank ravenously; Carados speculated that his visitor must have subsisted on dirty spring water and small berries for many days. Despite his hunger, however, the stranger was tall and muscular, with long blonde locks and pale blue eyes, and he bore himself gracefully.

After he had eaten and drunk his full, Carados asked the knight for his name and how he had come upon this remote mountain pass in the storm. And this is what the knight replied:

Thank you, my Lord, for your gracious hospitality, and may God in Heaven and His Son Who died to redeem us grant you many blessings and much good fortune. My name is Sir Claudin, and I am a knight of King Arthur's court. I have ridden forth from Camelot, like so many others, to seek the adventure of the Holy Grail—the blessed vessel with which Joseph of Arimathea had gathered the blood of Our Savior Jesus Christ as He bled for us upon the cross. The Grail is kept in Castle Corbenic, where it is watched over by the Fisher King, who suffers terribly from a wound, which cannot heal, and which renders him unable to walk or ride. Corbenic is shrouded in mist and enchantment, but I hope to find it and to look upon the Grail with my own eyes.

Carados replied: Sir Claudin, that indeed is a noble quest, but might I ask what you intend to do with this Grail? Are you riding for months through desolate country just to look at a cup, even one with lovely jewels? There are many other fine golden cups to admire in Camelot. Or so I am told.

Claudin laughed merrily. You have a fine sense of humor, my Lord. To look upon the Grail is to see Paradise itself—to be graced with a vision of Jesus Christ in all His Wonder and Majesty and Glory. To enter upon the adventure of the Grail, I, like all of Arthur's knights, had to swear off all lowly, earthly pleasures. I left my mistress behind in Camelot, and I have stopped in every chapel along the road to beg forgiveness from God for my many sins, especially my sins of the flesh with women. To achieve the Grail quest, I must be more than a powerful knight who can ride well and angle his lance. Sir Gawain, lover of many ladies—

 Barak A. Bassman

unrepentant, sinful lover of many ladies—has ridden forth to seek the adventure of the Grail but has won only humiliation and defeat. This is not for lack of skill or prowess—Gawain has triumphed at many tournaments over the finest knights in Christendom. No, he fails at the adventure of the Grail because his soul is stained with putrid sin.

It is the virgin Sir Galahad, who has never had an impure thought about a woman's flesh, who is winning fame far and wide for his glorious deeds in pursuit of the Grail. Poor sinner that I am, I can hardly compare to Sir Galahad, but I will strive with all my soul to atone for my misdeeds and, from now on, to devote my service to God alone.

I will ride forth again in the morning, after the storm passes, and seek out another priest, who perhaps will be kind enough to lend me a scourge and a hairshirt, so that I may mortify and punish my sinful flesh.

But for tonight, I thank you again, my Lord, for such generous hospitality. My body had grown weak over long days of wandering without food, and this fine stew and wine have helped to fortify me once more for the holy struggle that lies ahead.

Carados smiled, mumbled something cheerful about the goodness of God, and pushed more wine towards his guest. Sir Claudin drank again, a deep draught, and then said he was so weary that he needed to retire to sleep.

Later that night, as Sir Claudin snored loudly in his bed, Carados cut his throat and killed the questing knight. Such a fanatically pious man could only be trouble sooner or later; best to dispatch him promptly and seize his arms and horse.

IX. The Return of Morgan le Fay

MANY HAPPY, BOUNTIFUL years passed. Carados' lusts faded, and he was now drawn instead to sloth and gluttony, eventually growing a huge soft belly. His bastard sons had shot up like tall strong oaks and taken over the business of beating and robbing travelers on the roads. Carados was quite content with his life: he had founded a new noble house in this remote region, and, with their castle's great wealth, his sons would easily be able to bribe the Church to recognize their legitimate authority as Christian lords, naturally accorded to them by divine right.

He thought about what would have happened if he had not taken up the giant's challenge all those years ago. He would have remained a knight in King Arthur's court. He would have married a noble lady full of noble Christian sentiments.

He pictured in his mind how miserable his nights would have been with this devout wife. His peasant mistresses had clawed and writhed upon his body like agile, panting serpents in heat. But that would not have been the way with this highborn bride, no, she would have lied down rigid as a board, eyes tightly closed, as she braced herself for the repellant business of being impregnated. She would have doubtless prayed aloud to the Holy Virgin Mother for the fortitude to endure the ordeal of her husband's filthy desire.

Years of this sanctimonious drudgery would then have been followed by the Grail Quest, during which he would have ridden from hermitage to hermitage, flagellating himself, begging forgiveness for the sin of having experienced any meager scrap of pleasure, all in the hope that God would deem him worthy to gaze upon an ancient, rusted cup which was once used to store drops of Christ's holy blood. That last detail puzzled him: Why would anyone want to gather up blood in a cup?

Thankfully, the giant's challenge had freed him from this miserable fate. Given the true blessing of being an outlaw, he could now look back with satisfaction upon countless hours of rabid pleasure the likes of which the chaste knights of the Grail Quest could hardly imagine.

It was on a late summer afternoon, with the humid sun lazily wafting into his hall, that Carados indulged in such contented meditations upon his good fortune. His sons were out riding somewhere; his current mistress was sleeping off her too-large midday meal in a corner, her snoring breath scented with beer; and the lord of the castle was daydreaming, in blissful languor, upon a soft couch.

But then a sentry interrupted his idyll: My Lord, he announced, there is a lady at the gate. She says her name is Morgan le Fay, and that you will know what her business is. She seeks an audience.

Carados sat bolt upright. He had not seen the witch Morgan since she had abandoned him in the woods so many years ago. He had no idea what she could want now, or how she had found him, or how, for that matter, she had not long ago succumbed to old age and death. Still, she was a sorceress—one could never tell with such people.

Carados agreed to admit her into the castle.

When Morgan entered the hall, she appeared not to have aged a single day—the same long, thick red hair, the same lithe body.

Without getting up from his couch, Carados greeted her stiffly and asked what business had brought her to such distant parts.

She replied: My Lord Carados, I come to you as a penitent. I seek atonement for the treacherous part I have played in bringing to ruin the noblest court ever to have graced the land of Britain. I see now, too late, that I had foolishly abandoned the One True God and His Son, Our Savior Jesus Christ, for the lures of demons, and, as always, Lucifer's lies and temptations led only to death and despair.

Oh Carados, disaster has fallen upon Logres. Arthur and Lancelot went to war with each other. And while my brother Arthur was away waging his battles in Lancelot's lands, his bastard son Mordred raised a rebellion. When Arthur finally returned to Logres, with his forces ravaged and depleted, he was compelled to face Mordred's army at the Battle of Camlann. The fighting was terrible—almost every knight in Britain met his death there. Arthur slew Mordred, but Mordred still dealt him what should have been a mortal wound.

I saw my brother stagger off the battlefield, bleeding horribly. He lay down on a beach, watched the waves break, and seemed to be quietly settling his accounts with God.

When I saw him suffering so, my heart ached. After years spent blaming him for the sins of his father Uther and the enchanter Merlin, I finally understood, for the first time, his true nobility of spirit. I rode to him and put his barely alive body on my horse. Then I carried him to the seashore and summoned the fairy maidens, whose ship was fortunately nearby. They came swiftly, and I persuaded them to ferry Arthur to their merry isle of Avalon, the land of perpetual spring, where nothing can die, not even a man bleeding from deep wounds in his chest. Perhaps, over time, the wondrous fruits of Avalon will heal and restore him, and then, maybe, some day, he shall return to Britain—the once and future king.

But for now, Logres is in ruins. Thieves roam everywhere, taking what they please and violating the honor of maidens, because there are no more noble knights to protect the innocent.

The land suffers without its king. The trees bear no fruit, the grain no longer grows, and the livestock are afflicted with disease. The people are fleeing to other kingdoms, long lines of trembling women cradling hungry, wailing children to their withered breasts.

I at last grasped that my life had been devoted to the service of dark powers that had been plotting and scheming to scourge humanity with this misery and suffering. I had been blinded by my anger, and I had refused to let my ears hear the voice of God trying to reach me.

I had goaded and tricked my lover Accolon into fighting King Arthur. I had seduced other men of the court, too, and as I favored them with exquisite pleasures between soft sheets, I whispered words of sedition into their ears. I sowed discord wherever I went.

I also remembered you, my Lord Carados. It was I who caused your downfall and prevented you from becoming the great and heroic knight that you should have been. It was through my sorcery that I conjured the giant from Hell who journeyed to Arthur's court at the Christmas festival and set the challenge of the two reciprocal axe blows to the head. I had hoped to trick one of Arthur's knights into swearing gravely to submit to the giant's reciprocal blow in a year, and then to tempt this knight to break his oath—to show the knights of the Round Table to be cowardly and forsworn, men whose words and vows could not be trusted.

And you fell into my well-laid snare. Because of my wicked deeds, you were not there at Camlann to fight by Arthur's side and to protect him from Mordred's sword thrusts. Instead of growing into a noble and courtly knight, sheltering chaste maidens from danger, you were forced to become a violent brigand to survive.

But now is the time for us to redeem ourselves. What is past is past. Come with me back to Logres. Ride with your sons and your vassals. You can restore chivalry and honor to the land—God will then reward Britain with an abundant harvest once more.

Carados leaned forward and looked closely at the Lady Morgan le Fay. He saw how her eyes and hands trembled. He understood that she had spoken passionately from the depths of her heart, and that her remorse was genuine and consuming her soul.

Then he reclined back in his couch again and gave his response: a roaring laugh that erupted from the depths of his fat belly.

Other Books by Barak Bassman

Elegy of the Minotaur

Repentance: A Tale of Demons in Old Jewish Poland

King Solomon and Ashmedai: A Wisdom Tale

The Twilight of the Magical Siren: A Tale of Late Antiquity

The Leper Princess and The Court Jew

The Last Confession of Joseph della Reina

The Gifts of the Fairy Melusine

Necromancy of the Demon Maiden:
A Gothic Tale of Podolia

The Death of the Wizard Merlin

The Vampire and The Wandering Jew

The Emissary from Mezeritch: A Dark Hasidic Tale

www.ingramcontent.com/pod-product-compliance
Lightning Source LLC
Chambersburg PA
CBHW021742190726
48288CB00009B/3139